Bordertown Killer

Jay Hill Potter

A Black Horse Western

ROBERT HALE · LONDON

© 1955, 2003 Vic J. Hanson
First hardcover edition 2003
Originally published in paperback as
The Sundown Riders by Vern Hanson

ISBN 0 7090 7271 6

Robert Hale Limited
Clerkenwell House
Clerkenwell Green
London EC1R 0HT

Typeset by
Derek Doyle & Associates, Liverpool.
Printed and bound in Great Britain by
Antony Rowe Limited, Wiltshire

Bordertown Killer

It seemed as if everyone in Bravo had turned up to give Lucinda, Cal Mackey's bride-to-be, a very warm welcome when she arrived in town by stage. But it was not to be, for the stage pelted into Bravo with no driver, no guard and three dead passengers including Lucinda, who had been shot twice. Cal's life looked to be over.

Soon, though, revenge and hatred permeated Cal's brain and he and three friends from town formed a posse and headed out to San Antone. But the avangers soon ran into touble when the killers struck again.

Would Cal's burning desire for revenge and his brilliant skills with a gun be enough? He was going to need a lot of help – and luck!

CHAPTER I

Cal Mackey leaned against the tie-rail outside the Wells Fargo station and pared his nails with a Bowie knife. His feet hurt him in the new fancy-topped boots he had bought only that morning. He scuffed his feet in the dust. He caught himself writing a name in the dust with a shiny new toe-cap and looked about him covertly to see if anybody had noticed, before he obliterated the tortuous squiggle.

He put away his knife and loosened his neckerchief. This was new too, red silk with white polka dots. It made him sweat. He shoved the new white sombrero right off his head so it hung from its thong over his shoulder blades, the extra-wide brim protecting his back a little from the biting rays of the noonday sun. Everything he had on was new. The new vest was soaking up the sweat which threatened to ruin his fancy shirt, but the vest itself felt like it was made of horse-hair. He wriggled a little and muttered swear-words under his breath. It was not gentlemanly to scratch in broad daylight.

He turned his head as boot heels clattered on the

boardwalk behind him. Fin Bornwood grinned and winked. 'You look like you need a drink, Cal. Comin' in?'

'No thanks, Fin. I'm waiting for the stage.'

'I didn't think you were standing out here for your health,' said Fin, still grinning. 'The stage ain't due in for another ten minutes or so yet. You got time for one leetle drink.'

'I already had two drinks.'

The tubby Fin eyed Cal's rangy six-foot odd length and said, 'You've sweat that out by now. You got plenty room for another one. You stay here in the sun an' by the time the stage arrives you'll be melted away.'

Cal had to admit that Fin was doing some right figuring there. The saloon was conveniently next-door to the Wells Fargo office. Cal shrugged and followed Fin through the batwings into the cool gloom of The Fort Bravo. The saloon did not live up to its grandiose title but it sold good liquor.

The border town was called Bravo and it did not live up to its name either: Cal wondered what Lucinda would think of the one-horse burg when she got here. She did not have to like it particularly, however, for he was sure she would love the ranch which was to be their life together after they got married in Bravo by Cal's old friend, Brutus Calhoun, gunfighter turned preacher. The ranch was fifteen miles back and Lucinda would not have to come into Bravo again if she did not like the place. Bigger, lustier San Antone was almost as near, and on the railroad too, though on a different stage route.

This would be a big change for Lucinda after her sojourn back in the fancy East, but at least Bravo was a peaceful little burg and the folks here as friendly and hospitable as you would find any place in the West. No riff-raff here or fancy women like in San Antone. . . .

The thoughts sped through Cal's mind as he answered mechanically the jocular greetings that came from all sides. He had knocked back one tot of rye and had another cool glass in his hand before he began to realize what was going on.

The saloon had filled up since he had been in last. Folks had slunk in while he had stood out there at the tie-rail and sweat. Everybody was in their best clothes. Even Fin, a notorious saddle-tramp, had a brilliant new 'kerchief around his thick neck. This was a reception committee, Cal realized. The folks of Bravo meant to make his would-be bride real welcome. Cal suddenly got a thick feeling in his throat like he had a lump of steak stuck there or something.

'Where's your gun, Cal?' shouted one of the men.

'I left it home. I don't need no gun.'

'You'll need more than a gun, pardner,' said a bewhiskered oldtimer. 'Them female folks got teeth an' claws. Even the best of 'em has, son, take it from me.'

'The oldtimer ought to know,' chortled somebody else. 'He's been married four times.'

'I notice none o' you jackasses is wearing guns,' said Cal.

'We ain't getting married today,' said Fin.

A roar of laughter greeted this sally. Cal emptied another tot that somebody had cunningly inserted beneath his fingers. It was pretty lonely out on the ranch with only four Mexicans to help him. It was not very often he got into Bravo. The friendliness of the townsfolk, whom he had looked upon as a rather sober lot, now touched him deeply. The fiery liquor made him want to love everybody, to share his good fortune over a drink with them all. After all, it was not every day a man got married. And very few men were fortunate enough, particularly in this rugged land, to acquire a refined beauty like Lucinda.

The bewhiskered oldtimer was at his elbow now. 'Have one with me, son. Four times married.'

'What happened to your wives?'

'He wore 'em out,' yelled somebody.

When the laughter had subsided again the oldster said in an injured tone, 'That ain't so. You know it ain't so. When I got tired of 'em I fixed it so I could get rid of 'em.'

He began to tick off numbers on his horny fingers. 'The first one – her name slips my memory for the moment – I lost her to a fancy gambler in a poker game. She didn't mind – he was a mighty good-looking cuss. He thought he was smart. He didn't know I had stacked the cards against him. My, that filly shore was a hell-cat.'

The old man's wrinkled monkey-face puckered more than ever as he waited for the merriment to die down. He checked off another finger.

'Number two I remember well. She was a big Swedish blonde, the motherly type. A beautiful cook.

8

I put on four stone while I was with her. Cramped my style. I got up against a hornery cuss in a bar and got plugged in the shoulder because I'd lost my speed. I managed to kill the skunk, but it took me three shots an' it did my busted shoulder no good at all. Ingrid – yeh, that was her name – she smothered me. She wouldn't let me get out of bed with that shoulder. I lit out one dark night when she was out at the log-pile chopping wood for the fire. Then I met Sue, my third wife – or was Sue my fourth? I ain't quite sure . . .'

'You're a goshdarned bigamist!' shouted some-body.

The oldtimer held up his hand for silence. 'Do not interrupt, please,' he said loftily. 'I remember now, Sue was my *fourth* wife. The third one was named Lolita. She was a lot like Sue though, dark and ripe, only a full-blooded Mex instead of a half-caste one.' He turned towards Cal. 'What colouring's your girl, son?'

'She's dark.'

'An' purty?'

'Very purty.'

'Ah, them's the sort to keep a man's blood running freely when he ain't so young.'

'I'm young enough.'

'So you are. But I wasn't when I hitched up with Lolita. I didn't stay with her long – she had too many brothers and aunts and uncles and whatnot – you know what these Mexes are. I began to get stifled again. I had to kick one of her brothers' teeth in 'fore I lit out. But I figured that'd make 'em all hate

9

me more so they would talk Lolita out of looking for me. That was when I came to this territory an' met Sue. . . .'

The old man paused, making patterns on the wet bartop with a horny forefinger. Cal realized that the saloon had gone strangely silent.

'I was mighty fond o' Sue,' went on the oldtimer. 'She was half Indian but she was the finest gel I ever met in my life. She didn't stifle a man or nag at him or pester him with her relatives. . . .' He paused again.

The silence hung and stretched. Cal pushed a tot of whiskey beneath the horny fingers. 'What happened to Sue?' he asked softly.

'She got killed in a cattle stampede. She was coming out to meet me, bringing me a special pie she'd baked. It was my birthday. We found the pie. It had hardly been touched.'

The oldtimer knocked the whiskey back in one gulp. When he put the glass back on the bar, two large tears were running sluggishly down his leathery cheeks. Cal had that lump in his throat again. He tried not to look at the oldtimer too closely. The Fort Bravo rotgut was pretty strong; but well. . . .

The batwings flew open with a crash. 'The stage is in sight,' bawled a youth, then disappeared again.

Cal started away from the bar and almost fell over. His pins were kind of shaky, he must have drunk more liquor than he had realized. The oldtimer had him by the arm.

'Take it easy, son.'

Cal suddenly remembered what they called the

oldtimer. 'Thanks, Nevada,' he said.

'Come on then, or some o' these fancy galoots will be meeting your gel before you do.'

They joined the tide which burst through the batwings on to the boardwalk and turned towards the Wells Fargo station where the official in shirt-sleeves and green eyeshade stood waiting.

The sun made Cal giddy, so that at first he could not see the approaching stage. When he did so it seemed to him it was coming too fast down the bumpy trail and swaying from side to side. The Wells Fargo man had his watch out. 'He's ten minutes late,' he said. 'That's unusual for old Sam. Mebbe he's sick an' they got a relief driver on.'

'He's suttinly makin' up for lost time,' said somebody else.

Cal Mackey realized he had been in the saloon longer than he had thought – getting himself soaked with liquor when he should have been out here waiting. He wondered if he smelled too badly. He sunk his chin into his chest and inspected his clothes and flicked a few specks of dust from his shiny blue silk shirt. He wiped his face surreptitiously with the end of his 'kerchief and settled his white sombrero at a more becoming angle on his dark, close-cropped head. He tucked a few unruly locks, bleached yellow where the sun had caught them, beneath the wide brim.

He squinted at the stage again. It was, indeed, coming at a helluva bat. The passengers would be shaken up. He felt savage at the driver; the man should have gauged his time better instead of racing at the last minute like this.

From time to time when the four horses and the coach hit a soft spot in the trail they were almost hidden by a cloud of dust. A man came running back from the head of the street, waving his arms, his mouth yammering. And finally his words carried to the crowd at the Wells Fargo office.

'There's no driver on the box. Nor guard. Nobody at all. It's empty.'

The words were carried along. An ominous ripple ran through the people. Men began to leave the boardwalk and half-run, half-lurch up the street, most of them awkward in their high-heeled riding boots. Cal was amongst them and was dimly aware that old Nevada was still at his side. The crowd was broken up now, it streamed haphazardly. Some folks were on the boardwalk, some off it; those off it had to draw back quickly as the swaying coach thundered past them, enveloping them in dust. But not before the folks had seen the foam-flecked horses with staring eyes. The beasts, however, because they were so well-trained, pulled up only just past the office; almost opposite The Fort Bravo batwings, in fact.

Men ran from all sides, packing the forefront of the saloon in a solid mass. The coach looked intact, but there were no signs of human life about it. Cal Mackey came out of his trance and started forward, old Nevada at his heels. But the Wells Fargo man beat them both to it, blocking their way to the door of the coach.

He caught hold of the door handle and seemed to hesitate for a second. Then he turned the handle and flung the door open.

The girl fell out backwards and something like a huge tragic sigh came from the crowd.

Her legs were caught in something inside the coach and her skirts were draped decorously. Her white face was upside down, tragically beautiful with the sightless staring eyes. Her glossy black hair hung like a defeated banner in the dust.

A cry burst from the tight throat of Cal Mackey. A name! The name he had scrawled in the dust, the name he had spoken softly over again and again in the still of the night, the name he had seen written in the waving grass of the plain, in the sands of the desert, in the beautiful colours of the bluffs and the Western skies. . . .

A name he would remember for the rest of his life as he held the beautiful head and looked with staring eyes into the dead face.

CHAPTER II

They helped him to carry her into the Wells Fargo office and lay her on the couch. She had been shot twice in the breast and must have died instantly.

There were two more bodies, both male in the coach. But suddenly somebody shouted, 'Fetch the doc. One of these is alive.'

The doctor got there too late. The man had been shot in the belly but had one rational, painless moment before he died. He said that the stage had been held up by a bunch of five men. They had killed the guard and the driver and taken the strong-box. There had been four people in the coach. Three men and the lady. One of the men, a youngster named Larrabee, had leapt from the coach and torn the black 'kerchief from the leader's face. The leader had killed Larrabee. The leader was pretty young, pretty big, and before he had replaced the mask they had noticed he had a nasty white scar down his face reaching from his ear almost to the corner of his mouth.

The skunk had not taken any chances, however; he and one of the others had stood one on each side

14

of the coach and pumped bullets through the windows until they were sure everybody was dead. It was a miracle the story teller had lived as long as he had with two bullets in his stomach. He had managed to see through the window. The hold-up men had been riding across country, maybe in the direction of San Antonio.

Cal Mackey's horrified and grief-ridden daze soon turned to one of blind fury. He led the mob that ran out to saddle horses. Ex-gunfighter, preacher Brutus Calhoun, who should have performed the marriage ceremony, put in an appearance and nudged his horse to beside that of his friend.

The young man looked at him dully. 'This isn't your kind of business any more, Brute,' he said.

The giant preacher stroked his walrus moustache to hide his emotion. 'I saw your girl, Cal, and a man of God can also be a man of righteous wrath.'

Old Nevada spoke from the other side of Cal. 'I knew Brute in the old days, son. We might need him.'

Cal nodded, managed a wan smile and urged his horse forward. Across his bent back Nevada and Brute exchanged a look of pity. But Cal's sudden spasm of wretchedness did not last long and as they swept down the trail he urged his horse at an unmerciful pace. He had forgotten about the riders behind him, all he wanted to do was catch up with the people who had killed Lucinda and tear them to pieces with his bare hands.

The bluffs began to rise on each side of the road. 'It must've happened along here someplace,' said Nevada.

They turned a bend and saw the three bodies in the road, spaced out in a line as if tossed by a giant hand, left there callously. Already the buzzards were beginning to wheel in the yellow sky. The riders, over a dozen in all, clustered around the first motionless figure and Brutus Calhoun dismounted and turned the young man over on his back.

'That's Larrabee, I guess,' said tubby Fin Bornwood. 'He's little more than a kid. He certainly had guts – to attack an armed bandit the way that other fellah said he did.'

'That's Tim Larrabee all right,' said a middle-aged rancher called Mooney. 'He was my wife's cousin. He was comin' to Bravo to visit us.'

They moved on to the other two: Sam Rinaldo, the driver, and Jobey Kine, the guard, both grown old and wrinkled in the service of Wells Fargo. They had both been riddled with bullets. Jobey's shotgun had not been fired.

'They never had a chance,' cried Brutus Calhoun in a terrible voice. 'Not a chance!'

They carried the three bodies to the side of the trail and piled rocks gently around them to protect them from the buzzards. Then they split up into three groups to look for signs. The signal was to be two shots fired in the air.

Nevada, Brute and Fin accompanied the wild-eyed Cal, who said: 'I ain't wastin' time lookin' for signs. We know they came this way. I'm headin' for San Antone.'

The other three exchanged glances. 'Uh, you might have somethin' there,' said the sage Nevada. 'I

16

guess them skunks would have to get some chow an' stuff before lighting out for the hills or Mexico or wherever they wuz aiming. They'd steer clear of Bravo an' the other towns on the Fargo route. San Antone would be their best bet – a quick stop for provisions. They could split up there, too, if they wanted to, or hop a train. They could get a train into Mexico if they wanted to.'

'What are we waiting for?' said Cal savagely. 'Are you with me?'

Again the three men exchanged glances.

Brutus Calhoun said, 'I'm with you, Cal.'

Nevada said, 'Me too.'

'I got nothing particler to go back to town for,' said Fin Bornwood slowly.

They pushed their horses forward again, eased them into a gallop.

It was sundown when they hit San Antone. The first of many sundowns: of many visits to towns bawdy or quiet, hospitable or friendly. The beginning of a long and violent trail. . . .

CHAPTER III

San Antone, the hub of the Texas borderlands, terminus of the new Southern Pacific Railroad which reached in all directions. To Mexico, to the Pecos; to Houston, Waco, Forth Worth, Austin and other fabulous places of the frontier. A mixture of old Mexican, Indian and bawdy Western civilization, San Antone was a name on men's lips as they pushed to the frontier, a lodestar, a jumping-off place to a new civilization.

Fantastically-shaped adobe Mexican temples rubbed shoulders with clapboard honky-towns and bawdy houses. Shrouded beggars clustered on hollowed steps as old as time. Candles burned in the odorous gloom of the temples. Gringoes peered as they passed; but accidents would be liable to happen to them if they entered. Mexicans were everywhere, peons, dons, storekeepers. Swaggering cabalerros rubbing shoulders with Indians and half-castes in voluminous serapes or merely store trousers below their wiry copper torsoes; rubbing shoulders with cowhands, miners, carpet-baggers, gunmen,

18

gamblers, confidence men, tough frontierswomen and ladies of easy virtue. Indians sold curios to gawping Easterners; diminutive pimps plucked at sleeves and whispered coy words in bastardized Spanish.

The posse of four called at the nearest livery-stable and made their first enquiries. Nobody there had seen five riders. They left their horses to be rubbed down and fed. To the disgruntled Cal, Nevada said, 'We've got to rest the horses, son, an' fix some chow. Horses an' men can't go on forever without food and drink and rest. Besides, them ginks might be skulking here or might've been seen at the railroad station or something. We've got to make sure.'

'Yes, we have,' said Cal. 'Forgive me, folks, I guess I'm so eager to get sight of the skunks I ain't stopping to think straight.'

Fin and Brutus gave understanding nods. Nevada led the way along the boardwalk and turned into the biggest of the honky-tonks standing behind a garishly-painted false front that seemed to tower perilously to the very skies.

Over his shoulder he said, 'One good thing is, we've got an idea what we're looking for, but those jaspers don't know we're looking.'

The four partners found themselves in a huge high room illuminated by hanging kerosene lamps with crystal droppers. All along the back of the room ran a long bar with a brass footrail, battered and polished by countless boots. Right now there was not much of the footrail to be seen. At intervals stood brass spittoons half-full of sawdust; they had been kicked around a bit too. The backcloth of the bar consisted of ornate mirrors broken up by crude highly coloured paintings. The usual stuff: Custer's Last Stand; a buxom lady with a big feathered hat, a parasol and pink tights; a cattle stampede; a herd of buffalo drinking at a stream; more ladies in pink tights, some of them with their legs in the air.

The spaces which were not occupied by the ladies in pink tights and their human and bovine brethren were taken up by shelves holding every conceivable brand of snake poison. There was also, at the end of the bar, a large free lunch counter where, for the price of a couple of drinks, a man could eat as much salt pork, onions, crackers and corn bread as he could hold.

There was a small square of dance-floor and on this a few couples already jostled to the music of a piano, a concertina and a banjo played by three somnolent characters on a small raised dais. Unattached percentage girls stood on the edge of the floor like jackals waiting to pounce.

There were plenty of tables and chairs, plenty of grub being eaten, plenty of card-games being played. And, if a man wanted anything a little fancy there was one corner of the saloon taken up by highly-coloured gambling layouts presided over by hard-eyed gents in black broadcloth or equally hard-eyed ladies in smart abbreviated gowns. There was a huge garishly-coloured roulette-wheel, and layouts for faro, *monte*, 'chuck-a-luck', dice, keno, checkers and even, running at that very moment, a lottery with a fat pink sucking pig as first prize.

20

The four men sat at a table and ordered eats and coffee from a fat sweating waiter in a dirty white apron. Fin Bornwood said, 'Mebbe we ought to go an' see the marshal here. Mebbe he'll be able to help us.'

'The law,' spat Cal Mackey. 'The law was nowhere near Bravo when that thing happened. Where was Bill Penderson?'

Bill Penderson, sheriff of Bravo, was a pompous, slow-moving man. He and his deputy had been out chasing a Mexican horse-thief and probably had not got back yet, probably did not know about the stage hold-up.

'Bill was only doing his duty I guess,' said Brutus Calhoun gently. 'It was just bad luck that he wasn't there when he was needed most.'

'We don't need him,' said Cal, but his tone was not quite so vicious. Doubtless he realized there was truth in what Brute had said: Sheriff Penderson was an irritating sort of cuss but he had never shirked his duty.

'I dessay the stage hold-up is out of the jurisdiction of the San Antone law,' said Nevada. 'There ain't no stage line through here. However, the marshal might be able to give us a line on those jaspers – they might be well-known *road-agents*.'

Cal was silent now. He evidently did not think much of dragging the law into things. It was a bad sign, but none of his comrades could find it in their hearts to blame him. He only picked at his food and finally rose without a word and elbowed his way to the bar. His passage was pretty rough and many nasty looks were thrown after him. But he was big and lean and dangerous-looking; there was something about him that made people seek to give him a wide berth.

Fin Bornwood rose to follow him. Brutus Calhoun caught hold of the pudgy man's arm, saying, 'Let him go. Mebbe he wants to be alone for a while. Mebbe a drink will help to straighten him out. We'll step in if he goes too far.'

Fin nodded and subsided. The three men finished their meal, watching Cal all the time.

The tall, dark young ranny bellied up to the bar and took a drink from a sullen-looking barkeep. They saw Cal grab the man's arm as he was moving away again. The barkeep glared, but something he saw in the other man's face seemed to sober him.

Cal was talking. The man nodded; then shook his head; then shook it again. Then he moved along the bar and spoke to his colleague, nodding in Cal's direction at the same time. The second barkeep, a thin, pale character with a prominent adam's apple, went along to Cal and spoke volubly.

Cal nodded vigorously a couple of times. Suddenly the barkeep pointed. Cal turned and his partners saw his face. There was murder in it.

They followed the direction of his gaze. A man standing by the faro layout had intercepted Cal's glance too, and if he was not on his guard before, he certainly had reason to be that way now.

He was a stocky, hard-looking cuss with a red beefy face. Coils of tousled red hair escaped from beneath his pushed-back slouch hat. He looked the sort who could handle himself, but, as Cal started forward, he turned and disappeared through the batwings. Cal went through the crowd like a mad bull. His three partners moved to join him. But he had spotted something they evidently had not: the side door which led into the alley.

He was through it before they could reach him, for their progress was impeded by indignant folks, the backwash of his brutal charge.

Cal sped up the alley towards Main Street. As soon as he turned the corner he spotted his quarry. Then the stocky man disappeared from view on the opposite side of the street.

Cal crossed the street at a run and flattened himself against a log wall on the other side. Nothing happened. He looked out upon the street. People were tying their horses to hitch-rails, walking desultorily along the boardwalks, opening doors, spilling out yellow light from the places of entertainment before the doors were closed again. Windows blazed light blatantly: San Antone was a 'wide open' town. Cal was in a pool of shadow. Nobody paid any attention to him anyway.

Keeping close to the wall, he moved along the boardwalk until he reached the spot where the stocky man had disappeared. He found himself at the mouth of another alley.

He halted, debating with himself. His madness had turned to an ice-cold purpose. Maybe the skunk was lurking up there, gun drawn, waiting for him to show himself against the light at the mouth of the alley, waiting to blast him.

Thoughts sped through his mind. The thin bartender had been on duty when five saddle-tramps had entered the half-empty saloon early that day. They looked like hardcases and the one who seemed to be leader had been a big fellah with a scarred face. They had taken a couple of drinks apiece then left the place. It was much later that the stocky one had entered alone and started to 'buck the tiger'.

Though the stocky one could not have known that a member of the ill-fated stage party had been able to describe their leader, he was probably a wanted man anyway. Cal's murderous glance and his rush had been ample warning: now the tall waddy wished he had not been so precipitate. He looked back at the saloon and saw his three friends come out of it. He hesitated no longer but, crouching low, plunged into the alley.

Nothing happened. Feeling a little foolish, he straightened up, flattening himself against the wall. The alley was very dark. At the other end was the lighter hue of the night sky, a star here and there. Keeping close to the wall, Cal began to run.

He paused when he reached the top of the alley. He heard feet hit the hard sod at the other end. Evidently the boys had spotted him.

He turned the corner. The stocky man was limmed in the yellow light as he led a horse out of a small stable. He turned, his face snarling, and went for his gun.

Cal's gun was out of his holster when pain seared his arm and the weapon was jolted from his hand. As he staggered back against the wall, another slug tore

24

slivers from the wood. The stocky man forked his cayuse, thundered away.

Cal dived for his gun. His hand closed over it, but his fingers were sticky with blood and there was nothing to shoot at any more: horse and rider had vanished into the night.

He was resting stupidly on one knee when his companions joined him. 'He beat me to the draw,' he said dully.

'One of the hold-up men?' asked Nevada.

'Yeh.'

'You're sure?'

'I'm sure.' While he was quickly telling Nevada and Brutus what he had learned in the saloon, Fin ran from the stable. 'Not a single goshdarned horse left,' he exploded.

'We'll have to get our own,' said Brute.

'Nevada – you get Cal to the nearest doctor while Fin and me see if we can catch up with that rider.'

'I'm all right,' said Cal. 'It's just a scratch.' He was erect now, his sleeve rolled up as he tied up his arm with a 'kerchief. 'Just a crease. It numbed my arm for a bit that was all.'

The other three could see there was no use arguing with him. 'There's a pump in the stable,' said Fin.

Cal went in there to wash the blood off his hands while the others fetched the horses. Cal was thinking fast. For a time he had forgotten his grief; there was a job to be done. He wondered whether the stocky man's four pards were still in town or whether they were bivouacked somewhere outside and the fast-shooting jasper was riding to warn them. That was probably the case. With the stagecoach gold at stake the stocky man would hardly light out on his own, relinquishing his right to a share of the loot – particularly after he had got the drop on Cal so easily. Cal cursed at his own slowness. He followed his comrades at a trot. Fin had collected Cal's horse too. They mounted and set out at a gallop in the direction the stocky gunman had taken.

'He was probably sent into San Antone to reconnoitre, to find out if the stage job had been heard of here yet,' said Nevada. 'If he ain't got too much of a start he might lead us right to his friends.'

Cal realized that the other three had reached the same conclusion as himself. He hoped Nevada's last pronouncement proved true.

To live to avenge Lucinda was all he wanted now, and, if he lived no longer afterwards, well, that was all right too. The ranch was in the past: seemed like all he could do now was ride in the black night, hooves beating out the name Lucinda, Lucinda, *Lucinda*. . . .

A devil's tattoo, a paean of vengeance . . .

Twice they stopped to listen – while the voice thudded in Cal's brain. Lucinda, Lucinda, *Lucinda*. . . .

The second time Brute Calhoun said quietly, 'I heard a horse!'

The others listened – even Cal came out of his trance – but they could hear nothing. Brute, however, was reputed to have very sharp hearing. 'Come on,' he said. 'Don't take it too fast.'

They came upon the horse suddenly. He was grazing, riderless, his reins dangling. He nickered, moving towards the other horses as if he welcomed their company. He made a slight detour and suddenly the four humans realized why he had done this. On the hard-packed plain a man lay crumpled and motionless.

Cal Mackey was savagely alive again. He was first out of the saddle. He went down on one knee beside the motionless form and turned it over on its back. It was the stocky man.

Brutus made the examination while Cal leaned beside him like a figure carved from stone.

'Back's broken. He'll never be able to tell us anything or lead us anywhere.'

Cal Mackey rose, clenched his fists and shook them at the unoffending sky.

'Gopher hole,' said Nevada laconically, stabbing a finger. Gently he touched the young man's shoulder.

'Guess the fates played a dirty trick on us this time, pardner.'

CHAPTER IV

'Maybe the horse could lead us to the others,' said Nevada. 'Let him loose.'

Fin, who had been holding his bridle, let him go. The horse trotted a little way, then stopped and turned to see if his new-found friends were following. They set off after him. He went on again.

At times he seemed a little uncertain but, finally, led them to the warm ashes of a campfire. The fates, it seemed, had relented a little.

'They cain't have been gone long,' said Nevada. He dismounted and began to move in ever-widening circles around the ashes.

The old man was an ex-Indian fighter and an experienced tracker. The others stood watching him, not moving in case they obliterated anything.

Nevada disappeared into the night, only to come shambling back almost immediately.

'Looks to me as if they're aiming back for San Antone, or making a detour round it. Mebbe they got worried about that jasper we found an' are going back to look for him – it's a wonder our trails didn't cross.'

Fin Bornwood said: 'They weren't the kind who'd worry about a pardner.'

'Mebbe not. But don't forget that pardner could identify them and, if he got picked up, might have been liable to talk. Mebbe he had spent too much time at that faro layout back in the saloon. Mebbe he was long overdue here.'

'We'll backtrack,' said Cal. 'Lead the way, oldtimer.'

They did not meet a soul on their journey and approached San Antone from another direction. Despite the lateness of the hour some of the 'hells' were still snorting: there were parts of this lusty town that never slept.

'We better split up,' said Mackey. 'An' arrange to meet outside that big honky-tonk in an hour's time. If we hear any shooting we'll make straight for it, in case one of us is in trouble.'

'Right,' said Nevada. 'Have we all got the time?'

They were all in their best duds and wore their watches. Sober looks came over their faces as they remembered why they had dressed up this way. They made a great show of checking their watches, then they picked their directions and separated.

Cal Mackey rode his horse down the street and he heard the whistle of an approaching train. A glow in the sky betokened the location of the station. He urged his horse into a trot and made his way there.

San Antone rail terminal was a busy place, even at this time of night. Its yellow arc-lamps, its red, white and green signal lamps and the noise and the clamour and the jumbled shapes of trucks and coaches turned the place into an inferno. At first Cal, a plainsman born and bred, was a little awed by it all. Then he remembered the job he had to do and made his way to the siding as the incoming train roared down upon it.

As the train pulled up he saw the two men moving towards it. They were just shapes in the darkness. He urged his horse nearer but the beast reared, scared of the train. A man in a flat cap ran up quickly yelling, 'You can't bring that horse on here, mister.'

The man ran almost under the horse's feet, scaring him even more.

'All right. All right,' shouted Cal. He drew the horse back and tethered him to the tie-rail at the back of the platform. The train had stopped. The two men had moved nearer but they were still in darkness. Trying to appear nonchalant, Cal began to walk towards them. Having learned his lesson with the now-defunct stocky gunman, he was more cautious now. These two might be just innocent travellers – one of them carried a portmanteau – but, if they were not, Cal wanted to take them by surprise.

The signalman was already raising his flag. Although Cal knew nothing at all about railroad procedure, he suddenly realized that the train must be late or something and was having to move off right away.

He threw caution to the winds then, and began to move faster. The foremost of the two men had opened a carriage door and the light shone upon him. He was big and well-built. He climbed into the carriage and turned to take the portmanteau from his friend and Cal saw his face. There was a long white scar down one side of it.

Cal drew his gun and ran forward and at that moment the whistle blew. The man with the scar, the portmanteau in his hand now, looked up and saw Cal approaching. A startled look came over his face. He grabbed his companion by the arm and lugged him into the carriage and slammed the door. The train began to move off; Cal suddenly found his way blocked by the officious porter in the flat cap.

Cal waved the gun at him. 'Get out of my way,' he yelled incoherently. 'The two killers – they're on the train.'

The porter was a brave man. He ducked beneath the gun and drove his fist into Cal's stomach. The young man, taken by surprise, doubled up, but soon recovered himself and slammed the porter on the side of the head with the gun. The man fell limply.

The train was gathering speed. Cal raised his gun, then lowered it again with a curse. He became aware that railroad employees were converging on him from all sides. He looked down at the prostrate porter, realizing suddenly that, after all, the man had only been doing his duty. He delved into his back pocket, brought out some notes and tossed them in the general direction of the recumbent man. Then he turned and ran.

A bullet whistled perilously close to his head. Another chipped a lump out of the hitching-rail as he reached for the reins; then he was in the saddle, thundering away towards Main Street. He was almost blind with fury and frustration, so Fin Bornwood had to ride directly into his path before Cal spotted the tubby cowhand.

'What's eating you ? Have you seen somebody?'

'Have I seen somebody!' gasped Cal. 'Two of 'em. The one with the scar . . . getting on the train. I tried to stop 'em but got lit into by the station staff. They might be after me now.'

'Come on up the alley,' said Fin and led the way into the darkness beside San Antone's biggest honky-tonk. 'Did you find out what the train's next stop was?'

'I didn't have a chance. I had to slug a porter. His pals started to shoot at me.'

'That kinda puts a different complexion on things don't it?' said Fin. 'If them railroad people swear out a complaint you'll have the San Antone law on your neck. The best thing we can do, as far as I can see, is get to the law first an' state our case. Anyway, the marshal might be able to wire ahead and get those two killers picked up at the next station.'

For once, Cal was acquiescent. As they moved down the street towards the marshal's office he said, 'I only saw two of 'em get on the train. Mebbe the other two are still in town.'

'Mebbe they are,' agreed Fin. 'Mebbe they're still looking for their stocky pard who has so mysteriously disappeared – unless they found him on the trail, that is.'

'I don't think they would've done that, judging by the route they took back here anyway.'

As yet there were no signs of pursuit from the irate railway men. Cal and Fin halted outside the marshal's office and the latter rapped on the door. A gruff voice called 'Come in.'

The marshal of San Antone was, at that time, a hardbitten character named Charles P. Heckerstein, though he was known far and wide as 'Pecos Charlie'. He was a gnarled and heavy man of indeterminate age. He had a rich black moustache and a mat of greying hair on his leonine head. He had a peg-leg too, but that did nothing to impair his shooting powers. He was a gunfighter *par excellence*.

He was reclining in his swivel-chair with his feet on the desk when Cal and Fin entered. The marshal's eyes were drowsy as he eyed them, but his hand had fallen on to the desk-top very near to a Colt .44 shining dully in the light. 'What can I do for you gennelmen?'

Cal let Fin do the talking. For him the tale was too personal, too harrowing. Besides, he had not yet got over his near-miss at the station, the second near-miss in one night. A devil perched on his shoulder, leering at him; he was jinxed.

He took up the grim tale, however, when Fin got to the station part. The marshal listened without a change of expression, his face rather doleful behind his sombre moustache. When Cal had finished Pecos Charlie said laconically, 'I've often wanted to swat one o' them railroad men myself.'

'The train!' said Cal impatiently. 'What's its next stop?'

'Hold your hosses, son,' said the marshal and lugged a tattered timetable from a drawer. He ran a horny forefinger through the pages and finally pronounced, 'Laredo', and rose at the same time and went on, 'We'll go down to the dispatch office and I'll get a message through to the law there. After that we'll comb the town for those other two jaspers, who might be still here. Sounds like the Slack McGee gang to me – though they ain't worked round this territory in a coon's age – Slack McGee had a scar like that you told about an' he always looked young. Yeh, he must've been mighty young when he took to the owlhoot. Yeh . . .'

The marshal was still talking as he led the way from the office. A promise of action had stripped him of his indolence. The Colt .44 no longer winked dully on the desktop; it was strapped to Pecos Charlie's hip; his peg-leg went *thump-thump* purposefully on the boardwalk.

CHAPTER V

The telegraphist used his little 'clicker' and set the law of Laredo, on the very border of Mexico, on the lookout for Slack McGee – if it was, indeed, Slack McGee – and his friend.

Cal Mackey was torn between two things. He felt like riding pell-mell to Laredo with the hope of getting that scarred killer in his gunsight. But, then again, the other two hold-up men were quite conceivably still in San Antone, a much nearer target upon which he could vent his revengeful savagery. Besides, Fin and he were supposed to meet Brute and Nevada outside the big honky-tonk.

Marshal Charlie clinched things by assuring the young man that the law of Laredo, though rough, was a good law and would certainly take care of the two killers.

So they met Brute and Nevada, who so far had not turned up a thing. The marshal said things might be a little different now he had taken over. When he asked questions in San Antone people tried to find some answers. Cal told him about the lean barman

35

who had identified the stocky killer.

'We'll rope him in,' said Pecos Charlie and, forth-with, he did so.

'All you have to do,' he told the disgruntled barkeep. 'is keep your eyes peeled an' if you see one, or any of the five men, start pointing. Then run for the nearest cover.' He grinned wolfishly behind his whiskers.

The man's adam's apple wobbled. He nodded mutely. No stone was left unturned. The marshal led the way into more than one bawdy-house at the most inopportune moment. But it was in a stinking little Mexican cantina at the edge of town that they finally struck pay-dirt.

The lanky barkeep was so jittery by now that he gave the game away. He pointed a shaking forefinger and shrilled, 'That's one of them.'

The man was a half-caste who stood at the small zinc bar drinking tequila. He recognized the marshal and made a dive for the side door which was a feature of this kind of place: to facilitate the quick escape of any desperado who happened to have the law on his tail.

Brute and Nevada backed outside. Cal, Fin and the marshal fanned out, sweeping across the room, scattering customers before them. The fat Mexican owner watched wide-eyed from behind his bar. Cal Mackey lunged forward savagely as hammering hooves sounded outside. But the marshal was right by him and they hit the alley together, ran to the back of it. It was surprising how fast Pecos Charlie could move on his peg-leg.

He levelled his gun and fired. The horse squealed, throwing his rider, crumpling. Then, as Cal, Fin and Charlie ran on the rider rose to one knee. Tongues of flame blossomed; a gun boomed viciously. Pecos Charlie cried out a warning, then he too went down on one knee, fanning the hammer of his gun viciously until the half-caste was a mere shapeless bulk beside the greater bulk of his horse.

The three men were unhurt and went over to the dead man. 'Pity I had to kill him,' said the marshal. 'We would probably have been able to make him talk.'

Men streamed from the cantina, among them Brute and Nevada. 'The party's over,' boomed the marshal; and, in a quieter voice, 'This skunk's pardner must be somewhere around. Come on, Lofty: lead the band.' This to the lanky barkeep who was skulking in the background.

The body was dragged into the cantina and hidden in a back room. The fat proprietor was told to keep his mouth shut if he wanted to stay healthy. The law-party moved off.

Frustration was gnawing at Cal Mackey like an open wound. Two men killed; but his hand had not been the one to strike down either of them – beside the fast-shooting old marshal he was a mere unlicked novice – and nobody had talked. He asked Pecos Charlie if there would be word from Laredo yet. The marshal looked at his huge gold hunter watch and said the train did not arrive at the border settlement for another hour or more, even if it was on time.

The searchers traversed the whole length of town

again, in the hope they would run into the other road-agent. Maybe he was keeping on the move. It looked as if they were going to draw a blank: maybe, by now, the man had heard about his pard's violent death and had hit out for Laredo in the wake of the other two. That is, if they had not already divided the swag and split up for good.

All their surmising came to an abrupt end, however, at a sudden climax. They ran their quarry to earth with as dramatic suddenness as on the other occasion. The ensuing melee was something most of them would remember, tragically, too, until their dying day.

This time the lean barkeep held on to his quaking nerves. They entered a small gambling-house which they had already visited twice before that evening. It was kept by a tough white-haired old dame, known by the sporting fraternity the West over as Barbary Lil. She had been nurtured in the gaudy gin palaces of 'Frisco, the Golden Gate on the fabulous Barbary Coast. This ancient 'gilded lily' and the old gunfighting plainsman Pecos Charlie were firm, if rather ill-assorted friends. Lil let the lawman enter the place the private way, through her own rooms. They climbed the stairs and overlooked the gambling-hall from the balcony.

Beneath them was the small bar, covered with battered zinc. There were no customers along the bar, as in a saloon proper. A huge white-aproned waiter, an ex-pug called Louie, returned to the bar from time to time with his huge tray and a fresh batch of orders.

All the rest of the room, except for the narrow empty strip before the bar was taken up by every conceivable kind of gambling layout. There was even a city slicker in a loud check suit – Lil had picked him up half-starving in Austin – taking the suckers with a thimble-rig. There was the click of chips, the strained hum of the players, the croupiers' unemotional voices intoning the odds. Many of the croupiers and dealers were women – and Barbary Lil certainly knew how to pick her fillies. There was no music, however, and Lil did not permit liberties with her girls: this was a gambling-house and nothing more: if a customer entered with any idea in his head apart from gambling he was soon tossed out on his ear by Louie the Ape.

Cigarette smoke hung over the scene, and the law-party, with the barkeep. and the big white-haired old dame, had to take in things by sections. Then suddenly the barkeep's prominent adam's apple began to wobble as he gripped the sheriff's arm with claw-like fingers. He did not point this time.

'That man – that man over there,' he wheezed, 'thin, dark one using that faro layout by the door on the left. Red 'kerchief – black hat. I seen him with the one you shot – the half-breed . . .'

'You got a good memory,' said the marshal. 'But are you sure – are you absolutely sure?'

The barkeep nodded vigorously, his adam's apple bobbin' a mile a minute. 'Everybody tells me what a good memory I got,' he said with a sickly smirk. 'When I'm serving behind the bar I never forget a face. He came in with the other four but he seemed to be the half-breed's special pardner. I thought they looked like outlaws – I couldn't forget 'em. That's why Buster ast me when this gent here' – he indicated Cal Mackey – 'ast him.'

'All right,' said the marshal. 'Let's take it slowly this time. You stay here with Lil.'

The barkeep was quite content to 'stay with Lil'. The marshal led the rest of them down the stairs.

A fresh bunch of arrivals entered the gambling-house. A ripple ran through the packed smoke-blanketed throng. The law-party realized that maybe they were not to be allowed to take their time. People could not be trusted to keep their mouths shut: the news of the half-breed's death had been brought to the gambling-house. Also, they, who had caused that death, had been spotted.

'He's moving,' said Cal Mackey, lunging forward. 'He's making for that side door.' The road-agent, like his defunct pardner, had made sure he was near a means of exit: no doubt long years on the owlhoot had schooled them to this kind of caution.

Pecos Charlie, for all his age and bulk, moved quite as fast as Cal now, and the others were not far behind them. The law-party came helter-skelter down the stairs, broke out across the floor. The crowd fanned out before them; a chair went over; a man shouted. Cal drew his gun. 'Watch it,' shouted the marshal. 'You don't want to kill any innocent people.' Cal wagged the gun impotently. His eyes looked red with fury.

The thin dark owlhooter was almost at the door. He staggered a little, as if he had had too much to drink. He had the door open when something red and vital, spitting and scratching like a wild cat, closed with him.

It was the girl who ran the faro layout on which the road-agent had been trying his luck.

She was young, lithe, shapely, raven-haired. Her silk dress was low-cut, as well as being split down the skirt. Her brown legs flashed, her brown arms with them. The man was bewildered and temporarily stunned by the sudden attack.

With the savagery of his kind, however, he soon recovered and sent the girl sprawling – but not before she had slammed the door behind him with her foot. The law-men were getting nearer. People ran pell-mell to get out of the line of fire. Even as the road-agent wrestled with the door again, he drew his gun, turning like a wolf at bay.

'Watch out,' boomed Marshal Heckerstein. Almost simultaneously the outlaw fired: he was not so particular about the innocent people.

Fin Bornwood gave a queer choking cry and crumpled up. Even though he had not been in the forefront of the people the bullet, by some strange freak of chance, had found its mark in him. Another slug whined over the heads of gamblers and law-men alike. The road-agent was half through the now open door when Louie, the giant waiter, launched himself upon him from the side.

The man went down with Louie on top of him. In the sudden silence everybody near heard the sickening snap. It was over very quickly. When Louie rose he left the outlaw there in a strange unnatural heap.

'He broke his back,' whispered somebody.

Cal Mackey, bending over his tubby pard, Fin, heard the words as if in a dream. The third near miss – but that did not seem to matter so much this time: Fin's friendly eyes were glazing over. A froth of blood bubbled from the tubby man's lips and the happy-go-lucky, friendly eyes closed for the last time.

'You fools! You fools! I was getting him drunk. I would've had him there – helpless – if you hadn't . . .' It was the young virago in the red dress. But she halted her tirade now, as she saw the still form in the centre of the ring: 'I'm sorry,' she said. 'Sorry.' And her voice was suddenly much gentler.

CHAPTER VI

Cal ignored this crazy female. He bent and lifted the body of his friend, cradling Fin in his arms as if he were a child.

'Take him to my office,' said Pecos Charlie softly.

Cal gave no indication that he had heard but, carrying his burden gently, made for the door. Brutus Calhoun and Nevada followed closely in his wake. The marshal lingered. He turned to the faro girl and his voice had changed again when he spoke. It was not loud but the words dropped coldly and clearly, like ice water.

'Why did you want to get that man drunk, miss? Why did you attack him?'

'He was a member of the Slack McGee gang. I wanted to find out where Slack McGee is. I thought I could make that man talk. I have a score to settle with Slack McGee.'

'What score?'

The girl hesitated a moment, then said, 'I'll come to your office with you and tell you about it.'

Pecos Charlie shrugged. 'All right, miss.' He

turned towards Barbary Lil who stood nearby.

The gambling-house owner said, 'All right, Charlie, I heard what Biddy said. Carry on. Biddy's a good girl.'

Biddy acknowledged the compliment with a grave little inclination of her head. Pecos Charlie, who had an eye for a woman, noticed how beautifully-formed was her face and head, framed in the raven curls. Her nose was faintly aquiline, her eyes big and soft, her lips full, rich – they seemed to be trembling a little now, but her chin was firm. Pecos Charlie was an old Western gentleman, so he did not stare too hard at the superb figure revealed by the abbreviated gown. There was no skinny dance-hall pallor about this girl – Charlie figured she must do a lot of riding in her spare time – her face and arms were of a smooth, velvety brown.

'I'll get a coat,' she said, and sped up the stairs.

Barbary Lil looked quizzically at the old marshal. Charlie turned away from her and broke through the throng surrounding the body of the road-agent. He went down on one knee beside the corpse and began to search its clothing. A jack-knife, a dirty handkerchief, a pack of greasy playing cards, a sack of cigarette makings, a small roll of dirty banknotes and a handful of coins. . . . Evidently, the gang had not divided up or, if they had, this character had cached his loot someplace. The contents of his friend the half-breed's pockets had been no more profitable or revealing.

Charlie asked a couple of men to hump the carcase down to the undertaking-parlour. Then he returned to Barbary Lil.

Biddy came down the stairs, wearing a long coat which hid her dress. She led the way hurriedly. The marshal flipped his hand to the elderly dame and followed Biddy from the gambling-house.

Cal, Brutus and Nevada had already entered the office, the door of which, unless there was a customer in the jailhouse, was never locked. Cal had laid the body of Fin Bornwood on the bench beneath the window and covered it with a gaudily-beautiful Indian blanket. He had an idea Fin would not have objected to that blanket; the tubby little saddle-tramp had liked the bright and happy things of life.

Pecos Charlie, unfailingly courteous in the presence of women, did the honours.

'Gentlemen, I would like you to meet Miss Biddy . . . Miss Biddy. . . ?'

'Sanders,' volunteered the girl. 'Biddy Sanders.'

Each man shook hands gravely with her. All of them, except maybe Cal Mackey in his vengeful half-daze, wondered what she was doing there. The marshal pulled out a chair for the girl, then went and perched behind his desk.

'You can talk freely before these gentlemen, Miss Sanders,' he said. 'They're after Slack McGee too.'

Cal Mackey came out of his trance and started forward. 'What's she know about Slack McGee?'

He came to a dead stop as the girl turned and stared at him. Her dark eyes were a little indignant, a little puzzled. Cal realized he was becoming obsessed, boorish, making a fool of himself.

'I'm sorry, miss,' he mumbled. 'You go ahead.'

45

'Thank you.' She turned away from him, crossed her legs.

'Slack McGee killed my sister!'

The words fell flatly in the silence. The girl was evidently holding on to her emotions.

'How?' said Pecos Charlie, gently. 'Do you think you could tell us all about it?'

'Both our parents were killed in an accident six years ago and my sister and I lived together and worked in Galveston. We were models in a gown-shop. We showed off clothes for the customers and were quite happy together. Then one day Slack McGee came to the shop; although he did not call himself McGee then, he called himself Bennet. He was well-dressed, well-spoken. No doubt he was just hiding-out and enjoying himself with the proceeds of one of his robberies, but nobody could have suspected him of that. He let it be known by skilful hints that he was a Southern gentleman, that he had gotten the scar on his face in a duel, an affair of honour. They set great store by affairs of honour in Galveston.

'He came to the shop with a local Creole beauty who professed to be his cousin. There was quite a lot of scandal about them, but, because Mr Bennet was a 'Southern gentleman', he was looked upon very indulgently by the ladies of the town. Many of them were fascinated by him, they thought him mysterious, a little dangerous. My sister, Mary, was no exception. Mr Bennet spent a lot of time at the shop and finally began to come alone, without the Spanish beauty. There was a rumour that they had fallen out. I began to realize that Bennet was coming to the

46

store solely to see my sister and myself, or, rather, my sister mainly. I gave him no encouragement; I mistrusted the man.

'It was some time before I discovered Mary had been going out with him, but, because she knew I didn't like him, she had kept the fact a secret from me. I am a couple of years older than she was. Her association with Bennet was the first real secret she had kept from me, that was the extent of her infatuation. I told her she was a fool, that the man was no good to anybody. We had our first really serious quarrel. Two days later, during the night, Mary sneaked out of our lodgings and ran away with Bennet.

'Finally, about a month later, I managed to trace them to a little settlement about ten miles from Galveston. The place had an unsavoury reputation. I found Mary in a tumbledown little clapboard hut. Bennet had left her and she had discovered she was going to have a baby. She had also found out who her lover really was, Slack McGee, outlaw and killer. A law-man had tried to take him there in the settlement. McGee had killed him and run away. Mary had no idea where he had gone.'

Biddy paused, a little breathless. The men waited in silence, grave-faced. They knew this was not just a whining hard-luck story. They had not expected a gambling-house girl to talk this way. She was obviously far better educated than any of them. She went on:

'Despite all McGee had done to her, my sister still loved him. She was sick. I had her moved from that dreadful settlement and went with her further West,

47

to Austin, where there was little danger of any of our old friends finding us. Mary could not have faced them . . .'

Biddy's voice suddenly began to break. 'She was almost out of her mind. I had to watch her constantly. Finally, our money ran out . . . I got a job as a croupier in a casino in Austin . . . I paid for a nurse to look after Mary. The woman was not very efficient. She let Mary get hold of some stuff . . . Mary poisoned herself. She was dead before I got home. . . .'

There was a little gasp from one of the listeners. Then, in the silence, the girl's words fell flatly again.

'Slack McGee killed my sister just as surely as if he had put the muzzle of a gun to her head and pressed the trigger. I made up my mind I would find him and kill him. I heard a rumour that he was in the border area, so I came here and got a job in the gambling-house. Mrs Tyler has been very good to me.'

The sheriff blinked. He had never heard Barbary Lil called 'Mrs Tyler' before. Biddy went on talking:

'The day before yesterday I saw McGee and four other men riding through town. By the time I had got a horse they had gone. I remembered the faces of some of McGee's friends. That was one of them who Louie killed tonight. I was letting him win, getting Louie to give him plenty to drink. I thought if I got him pretty helpless I might get him alone and make him talk.'

'That was a pretty big consignment for a young lady,' said Pecos Charlie gruffly.

'We all admire your courage, miss,' said Brutus Calhoun.

Nevada and Cal made murmurs of assent. The girl said, 'Thank you, gentlemen. Now perhaps you will tell me your story. If you're after Slack McGee I would like to be able to help if I possibly can.'

Cal Mackey took it upon himself to tell the story this time. He did not look at the girl; or at anybody else, in fact. He spoke as if he was saying a previously rehearsed piece: bald facts, no emotion, no explanation.

When he had finished the girl said softly, 'I'm sorry.'

Then Cal was speechless, could only duck his head. He suddenly realized that he had not expressed his sorrow about the tragic death of Biddy's sister. He had been too wrapped up in his own grief. His heart swelled with savagery. He was a poor apology for a man, he told himself; this girl had more guts in her little finger than he had in the whole of his long, tough, rangy body.

There was a knock on the door and it was flung open. A diminutive boyish edition of a glorified saddle-tramp stood there and carolled, 'Marshal, there's a message comin' through fer you at the tele-graph-office.'

'This is it, boys,' said Pecos Charlie. 'You better come along too, Miss Biddy.' As he led the way from the office he flipped a coin to the grinning little cowpuncher.

The telegraphist was just finished taking the message. His expression was glum as the coder rattled alarmingly.

'Nobody answering to the description of Slack

49

McGee got off the train at Laredo. The train was almost empty. There was no big man with a scar – no two men, one of whom carried a suitcase . . .'

Pecos Charlie, his face fiery, opened his mouth to speak. The telegraphist held up a warning hand. 'Wait a minute. . . .

'. . . Two men were seen to leave the train when it slowed down on the bend at Crimson Buttes. They disappeared among the rocks . . . that's the lot.'

'Where's Crimson Buttes?' asked Cal Mackey.

'About halfway between here and Laredo,' the sheriff told him. 'It's just a huge outcrop. When the sun catches it, 'pears like it's washed in blood. That's why it's called Crimson Buttes.'

'Mebbe those jaspers had got that move figured all the time just in case sort of,' said old Nevada. 'Mebbe they had horses stashed among them rocks.'

'Must've had,' said the sheriff. 'Otherwise they'd have a mighty long way to walk before they got to any habitation. Mebbe they were figuring to doublecross their pals as well as everybody else.'

'What are we waiting for?' said Cal Mackey. 'Let's hunt sign.'

'Yeh, I guess those two skunks won't just wait for us to catch up with them,' said the marshal. 'Everybody get their horses. We'll meet back here.'

For a moment Miss Biddy Sanders was almost forgotten. But she turned up on her horse like the rest of them.

'This ain't woman's work,' said Pecos Charlie.

'If you forbid me to come I shall follow you,' the girl retorted. 'You wouldn't want me to get lost would you?'

'No,' said the marshal. 'You armed?'

'I'm armed,' she said.

They were already moving. The girl rode beside the old law-man. 'Can you shoot straight?' he asked.

'I can shoot straight. I practised a lot.'

'Seems like you got me buffaloed, gel,' he said, and there was a hint of laughter in his voice.

CHAPTER VII

They reached Crimson Buttes and old Nevada hunted sign by the light of a lantern Pecos Charlie had thoughtfully provided. The old Indian-fighter tried to shield the light as much as he possibly could as he hunted in the fantastic outcrop.

'They had hosses here all right,' he said. 'Either they have stashed them beforehand or somebody else brought them here for them.'

The little group of horsemen, with the girl in their midst, watched the light bobbing away from them until it disappeared among the rocks. Pecos Charlie and Cal Mackey dismounted and set off in opposite directions, leaving Brutus Calhoun with Biddy. Looking down as they climbed they could see the ribbon of the Southern Pacific shining in the pale moonlight. It was surprising how nimble Pecos Charlie was despite his peg-leg.

They lost sight of each other but converged to the centre again as Nevada whistled cautiously.

The old Indian-fighter had rejoined the preacher-gunman and the girl. His lantern rested on the

ground. He said, 'I've found the tracks leading out.
Not aiming for Laredo, not aiming for San Antone.
Not unless them jaspers intend to make a wide
detour, that is. Where else they could be aiming for
I'm not quite sure, unless it be a quiet spot on the
border. It's a mighty long way to the border in that
direction howsomever and they'd have to get over
the worst part o' the Rio Grande. I don't think they
stopped to light a fire. They must be aiming to
bivouac somewheres ahead.'

'I didn't find any ashes either,' said Cal.

'Neither did I,' said the marshal. 'But I found
something else which may be a clue.' He opened his
palm and something gleamed there. 'It's part of a
Mexican rowell. It's new an' it ain't been there long.
I figure one of them jaspers snapped it off his boot in
the rocks without knowing about it.'

He pushed the little tortuous-shaped piece of steel
carefully into his vest pocket. 'It's getting late. Do we
ride till dawn?'

'You're the boss,' said Cal Mackey.

The rays of the lantern on the rock floor threw a
ghostly light only on the lower regions of men and
beasts. The marshal was looking upwards at the girl,
up there on her horse in the shadows, her face only
a pale blob. She said:

'Let us ride, marshal. If you're uncertain about me
there is no need to be. I'm a good horsewoman and
I can stand the pace.'

'I guess there wasn't any need to ask,' said Pecos
Charlie softly. 'All right, let's go.'

Nevada picked up the lantern, blew it out, hung it

over his saddle-born. The three men mounted, joining Brutus and the girl. The little cavalcade with the cat's-eyed Nevada in the lead, made their way cautiously out of the Crimson Buttes and into the terrain beyond, a mixture of sand, rock and dry, brown grass.

A little wind moaned a melancholy dirge. There were no stars and the moon was very pale, so that the riders could not see far in any direction around them. For all they knew the two road-agents – and maybe a third – were in hiding out there, waiting for them. Three dry-gulchers with guns and the element of surprise on their side could mow down such a small party as this. Probably this was why Pecos Charlie advised them to spread out a little and Brute Calhoun kept his protecting black-clad bulk in front of the girl.

Brute was pretty silent. In fact, he had not talked much at all since the Bravo party hit the trail in the first place. Gone was the rhetorical giant who had charmed the faithful with his silver tongue or lashed the unbelievers with scorn. Gone was the humorous twist of the mobile lips beneath the walrus moustache, the kindly twinkle of the level grey eyes. These now were blotted out, smoothed over by the features of a poker-faced gambler, a steel nerved gunfighter who had counted the odds, who had a job to do and meant to finish it without unnecessary gab. There was little need for talk. In this case, though it may have saddened Brute's preacher conscience somewhat to realize it, his comrades did not need to be talked around to his point of view – when men are vengeful and full of righteous justice they need not the preacher, only the fighter.

Nevada did not relight the lantern but they stopped from time to time and he took a chance on flaming lucifers to hunt sign. They were still on the trail, he said. At first he had not been quite sure that there were three horsemen, but now he was certain. Somebody must have delivered the horses at the Buttes. Maybe another member of the gang. Or maybe a Mexican or Indian contracted to lead them over the border or into some secret hideout.

'Mebbe they're making for the Pecos,' said the marshal. 'Slack McGee's well-known up there – the law wants him. But he's also got plenty of friends.'

The sky became washed with a pinky-grey light, the first signs of approaching dawn. Then the full dawn came suddenly, like thunder the way it does in these harsh, barren and beautiful border-lands. Rainbow colours flushed the Western skies, their delicate reflections were chased across the rocks and the grass, and were blazoned upon the cactus and the stunted trees. The distant hills at the right-hand side of the riders were like the borders of a fairyland. Up ahead, across the flat immensity, was the cool suggestion of a mirage and they knew that they were riding towards that fabulous river, the Rio Grande del Norte.

The riders stopped. The marshal swept out a hand. 'That way lies the Pecos, in the other direction the hills. Mebbe you're right about 'em not making for the Pecos, Nevada, where there's a risk of 'em getting boxed in by the law. But what do you think about the hills?'

'Right now them hills look mighty purty,' said Nevada. 'But I know better. I prospected 'em when I first came to this part o' the West. I didn't get enough gold to fill a hollow tooth; just sunstroke, an' blisters, an' a belly like a buzzard's neck. If those skunks know this territory – and I figure at least one of 'em does – they won't take to the hills. And, believe me, beyond them hills it's even worse: a reg'lar devil's badlands. No, I think they're making for the Rio. All the signs seems to point that way. Take it slow gents . . . take it slow.'

'We'll never catch up with them if we take it slow,' retorted Cal Mackey, in whose heart savage impatience had begun to grow again.

'Nor if we go like bulls at a fence an' miss the trail,' rejoined Nevada imperturbably.

Cal knew he had spoken out of turn. He felt the eyes of the others upon him, particularly those of the girl. He felt himself flushing. 'All right, let's keep trailing,' he said with unwonted harshness.

Nevada spat a stream of tobacco juice into the dust, grinned and led the way. Brutus Calhoun suddenly spoke up.

'I know the section of the river up ahead. A posse chased me there once. There used to be a Mexican settlement and a landing stage. Plenty of boats too – though the Mexicans charged a small fortune for their use to anybody who seemed extra keen to get to the other side of the border. In those days the settlement was ramrodded by a Mexican called Verez. He ran a combined saloon and store. If he's still alive he must be pretty old.'

Miss Biddy was looking at Brute in amazement. She probably thought it strange that this big distinguished-looking man had ever been chased by a posse. She had not been told he was a preacher, but his clothes and voice rather gave him away. They had not spoken much together, but he had been very gentle, attentive and protective towards her – much more so than any of the others – and she had had plenty of time to study him. She must have wondered more than once why he was taking part in this kind of chase.

Nobody enlightened her. But Pecos Charlie said, 'I heard about Verez. Just rumours. He is – or was – quite a character I gather. Maybe the settlement's finished, though.'

'Maybe,' said Brute and lapsed into silence again.

Nevada had dismounted from his horse and was walking carefully ahead, half stooping most of the time. Nevada's eyes, despite his age, were very keen and well-trained. He had had his training with Dog Soldier scouts during the Indian wars. He read a story in a broken blade of grass, an upturned leaf, a mark in the dust, a scratch upon a rock.

'They came this way all right,' he finally pronounced. 'Still three of them, unless I miss my guess. One of them with an unshod horse.'

'The guide maybe,' said Pecos Charlie. 'An Indian?'

'Could be,' said Nevada as he remounted.

They rode on into the glory of the early morning

and the sun began to find them out.

A mirage danced before them of cool water and green grass. The grass along the Rio in this part of the territory could not possibly be that green, said Nevada. The mirage might be a reflection of a scene far away in the Gulf of Mexico. Sunshine and water played funny tricks: many a man alone in the barren lands had been driven crazy by them.

Cal Mackey happened to glance at the girl. She had not turned a hair. She looked cool in her white shirtwaist and riding skirt, with the big wide-brimmed brown sombrero on her black curls. She was brown and healthy and wholesome-looking, not at all like the conventional idea of the fast-living saloon girl.

He had not had much to do with dance-hall or gambling girls. During the war the neck of the woods he had fought in had not seemed to contain women of any kind. And since he came back from the war he had been too busy scrabbling a living for himself among the rest of the returning 'heroes' to bother about women. He was not a lady's man and had never bothered about them until he had met Lucinda during that short trip to visit the finance company on the edge of the East.

Thoughts of Lucinda came rushing back to him. He wondered what she would be like were she with them now. She would not be able to stand these conditions. Then he realized that she could never be with them and, were it not for her loss, they would not be here anyway. The sadness welled up within him again. He did not look again at Biddy and rode head down; he might have been completely alone with his thoughts.

The sun began to get stronger, to drip its heat upon horses and men. Finally the cavalcade paused in the shelter of an outcrop of rocks, one of the clusters which embellished these wastes, tossed down there without rhyme or reason as if by a giant hand. The four men and the girl partook of the provisions they had brought with them from San Antone. They used their canteens sparingly, taking a drop of water each for themselves, then laving their horses' noses with bandannas dampened for the purpose. The beasts seemed to get a certain amount of sustenance from cropping the short brown grass.

The cavalcade rested briefly before pushing on at a faster pace, for by now Nevada was sure of his direction. A wind had brought up a bright and good freshness with it. The horses needed no urging now: they had smelled water, though Nevada said the Rio was many, many miles away yet.

The horses travelled at a steady lope. Biddy's mount was a little pinto with the stamina of a cowpony. The girl rode well: beast and rider suited each other and did not seem to be getting in so much of a lather as the rest of the bunch. The pinto was still frisky, rolling a wicked eye, and its rider was as brown and wholesome and sweetly cool-looking as an autumn nut.

The morning passed and part of the afternoon and the sun swung over their heads like a highly-polished brass gong. No horse could stand the pace forever and finally Pecos Charlie said, 'What do you think, Nevada?'

The old man said: 'I figure we ought to be in sight of the Rio soon. Mebbe we ought to rest up for a while, light a fire and boil some coffee. Then we can approach the river by night in case those jaspers are lying low. Mebbe they don't know we're following them, but I don't expect they'd take any chances anyway.'

Charlie said grimly, 'No, Slack McGee's a hellion but he isn't the kind to take a chance unless it's gonna pay off. That's why he's been able to raise hell for so long and with such success.'

The cavalcade dismounted. Almost immediately the two youngest members, Biddy and Cal, began to hunt wood. Biddy, her arms full of dry miscellaneous bits and pieces, came face to face with the young cowboy. She saw sudden friendliness flare in his eyes, only to be replaced almost immediately by that look of old sadness. Not so very old really; she pitied him, lowering her eyes as she led the way back to the big rock overlooking the hollow which had been chosen for the camping-place.

Although she quickly tried to disguise it, Cal had seen that look of pity. It enraged him, but he was not sure at whom his rage was directed: at her or at himself. He knew for sure, however, that he did not want pity. Most of all he did not want this girl's pity; although they were so dissimilar in every way she reminded him, strangely enough, of Lucinda. What was he, he asked himself, a man or a yellow dog? A real man should be able to rise above all things.

Old Nevada lit the fire and the girl prepared coffee and flapjacks. Afterwards while they smoked – all of them except Biddy and Brute that is – Cal acted quite normally, joined in the desultory conversation.

The sundown blazed. Slowly waned. A blood-red peace fell over the land, a little chill wind blew.

Red. Another vengeful sundown. Leaving behind it a flush of blood in the sky.

'Let's ride,' said Cal Mackey.

CHAPTER VIII

Manuel Verez, though old, was still very much alive. Even as he sprawled on the wicker chair on his veranda in the late afternoon, there was a hint of latent power in his stringy body. Verez had turned seventy long since and his long years in the sun and the wind of the savage border-lands had made him as tough, as supple and as brown as a rawhide whip.

Such a rawhide whip, almost as old as Verez himself, was looped over the veranda rail within reach of his hand. The old man's rifle was behind him, leaning against the cabin wall. He had many friends – but he had many enemies too. He was just and he was ruthless, the watchword of him and his kind must be eternal vigilance. Eternal vigilance, coupled with co-ordination of a fit body and a fit mind had kept him alive, and he hoped would continue to do so. And when these things no longer were possible he wanted to be shot like the worn-out old dog he would surely be.

He had left his mark on the border and in Mexico on the other side of his beloved Rio. His songs would continue to be sung after he had gone, his legend would grow. Verez was somewhat of a poet, somewhat of a philosopher but, withal, a ruthless realist too. He preferred to be a 'living' legend for as long as he possibly could: he took pains to protect his dubious immortality.

From his veranda he could look to the right of him at the Rio sparkling in the sunlight, to the left at the cluster of adobe huts, log cabins and clapboard shacks that made up the settlement. Out in front was the immensity of the arid plain, the blue hills in the distance, the outcrops, the cacti, the buzzards in the yellow sky. At that moment Verez could indeed be said to be monarch of all he surveyed.

His cantina and stores, though not particularly large, was by far the most imposing building in the settlement. He had plenty of staff too, in the building itself and out of it. Many just peons born to bow and scrape; others fighting men ready to rally to his side whenever he called. Sometimes they rode on the side of the law, sometimes outside of it. Verez was not always in agreement with other men's laws, so he made his own. He had plenty of scouts out, too. He knew what was going on. Though he did not resemble a spider in any way, he could be likened to one, spinning his intricate web on both sides of the border, interfering sometimes, for good or ill, in the lives of people who did not even know of his existence – or thought the old buzzard had been dead for years.

Down by the landing stage the boats rocked gently; the waves made little slapping sounds against their sides. From the living-quarters behind Verez came the somnolent *whisk-whisk* of a broom. The Indian youth, Matu, was doing his chores. It was almost seventeen years now since Verez, on one of his pillaging raids, found the Indian baby beside the fever-stricken bodies of his mother and father.

Verez had no wife, no kith or kin. If he wanted a woman there were many to fall at his feet. He was like one of the old Dons of his fabulous past who could take a concubine from the family of any of their followers. He had taken the Indian boy in his home and now treated him almost as a son. Matu's single-minded worship of the old man was a touching thing to see. The strong, handsome Indian youth would have willingly laid down his life for 'the master', as he called the old Mexican.

The gentle sound of the brush was very soothing in the hot, still air. Verez's eyelids drooped, but he jerked erect when the sound ceased and Matu came out suddenly upon the veranda.

'Riders coming,' the Indian boy said laconically in his deep voice.

'I don't hear anything,' said Verez. He shaded his eyes with his hand. 'I don't see anything either . . . I must be getting old.' He chuckled, knowing the Indian youth had the hearing and the eyesight of a hawk.

'Wait,' said Matu. They waited, then he pointed. 'Three riders.'

'I see them now,' said Verez. 'I wonder who they can be.'

There was a slight pause before Matu said, 'The

halfbreed, Piute Joe . . .' Matu leaned over the veranda rail, shaded his eyes to peer into the sun. 'Slack McGee . . . I do not know the other one.'

Verez frowned but made no comment. He glanced over his shoulder at his rifle then reached out and gently grabbed the rawhide whip from the rail and dropped it over his knees. Matu watched him with dark liquid eyes.

Verez said: 'Go on with your chores but keep near.' Matu nodded his head gravely. 'Yes.' He moved soundlessly back into the house. Verez pulled his wide-brimmed hat over his eyes, slumped into a more somnolent attitude than ever and waited for the horsemen to arrive. His lean brown fingers caressed the handle of the rawhide whip across his lap.

He did not look up as they dismounted and looped their horses' reins over the hitching-rack. He watched them from beneath lowered lids and did not raise his head until the dark wizened little man with the evil face had one foot on the steps. Then he barked:

'Stay where you are, Piute Joe.'

The man stopped dead, licked his lips. The two men behind him halted too. The big one with the scar and the lean one with the pale, sick face.

Piute Joe said: 'I thought you were asleep, Manuel. I have brought friends.'

'I know one of your friends,' said the old Mexican tonelessly.

'Hallo, Verez,' said Slack McGee. 'Long time no see.'

65

Verez ignored him. The old Mexican was still look-ing at Piute Joe. 'My cantina and stores are open for business if you wish anything. You will use the door around the corner, please.'

'But you don't understand, Manuel. These gentle-men have business, real business.'

'I know their business. They have government money and they wish to dispose of it.'

'Hey, how did you know that?' The lean sick-faced man spoke for the first time.

Verez did not look at him but said, 'I get to know things.'

Piute Joe licked his lips again, grinned with yellow snaggle-teeth. 'Manuel gets to know things all right. It's not like you to turn your nose up at government money, Manuel.'

'You're a skunk, Joe,' said Verez tonelessly. 'I do not like your friends – I did not tell you to bring them to me.'

Joe pretended not to hear the insult. His tongue was snake-like. He said, 'But you don't understand, Manuel. This is the biggest haul.'

'I know all about the haul. I know how it was taken. I know there was a lot of unnecessary killing and one of the victims was a woman. I do not do business with people who make war on women. Take your foot off that step, Joe. Go! And take your friends with you.'

Slack McGee started forward, but was brought up short by Piute Joe's outstretched arm. The half-breed said, 'But look, Manuel. . . .' He began to climb the steps.

Verez rose with one smooth uncoiling motion.

The whip in his hand cracked. With a cry of pain Joe started back, his hand to his face. He would have fallen down the steps had not Slack McGee caught him. Blood began to well sluggishly through his fingers.

Half-covered by Piute Joe, Slack McGee made a quick movement; then, just as quickly, froze in his tracks. Matu stood on the veranda now and negligently in the crook of his arm he held a sawn-off shotgun. Maybe the sick-faced hombre, being at the back, did not spot Matu as soon as the other two did. Anyway, he made a fast movement too: his gun was out of its holster when the Indian youth's weapon boomed. Slack and Joe flinched instinctively as the shot whistled past them. Their trigger-happy comrade screamed with pain. His gun made a parabola in the air and hit the sod. By that time the sickly-looking man was down there too, writhing as he clutched at a mutilated shoulder, vainly attempting to stem the flow of blood.

'You will do as the master says,' intoned Matu.

Verez had not moved. His whip still dangled in his hand.

Slack McGee said, 'You won't get away with this, Verez. Or that young Injun devil. I'll . . .'

'You'll go an' get what you want from the store,' put in the old Mexican. 'Because I am a patient man I will still allow you to do that. You can doctor your friend too; he looks as if he needs it. My storeman will see to these things for you. I would not advise you to be hasty with him, however. He is not a patient man, a *caballero* who lost one arm when young in a knife-duel. This has soured his disposition just a leetle.'

McGee began, 'I came here to do business. I . . .'

'Maybe it is best you take their guns, Matu,' said Verez. He reached behind him and took up his rifle, pointed it negligently in the direction of the three men.

Piute Joe still caressed his cheek where the thong of the whip had made a livid slash. The burly Slack was obviously beside himself with fury, which swelled with every minute as he realized he could not do a thing. That old greaser on the veranda could shoot a fly off a fence at a hundred paces. The third member of the ill-assorted trio had lost all interest in the proceeding. His hand still clutched to his messy shoulder, he lay in a crumpled and inert heap.

Still holding the shotgun expertly in one hand, Matu vaulted the veranda so that he would not get in the line of fire. He came up behind Joe and Slack and relieved them of their hardware.

He then bent over the prostrate man.

'Is he dead?' asked Verez.

'No, he has passed out only.' Matu seemed hugely amused by the fact. He was a full-blooded Apache and although he had adopted the ways of the white man, he still had many inherently Indian traits. The Apaches have in particular a very ribald sense of humour. Matu was evidently no exception. Slack McGee turned angrily towards the youth.

'Careful,' warned Verez.

But Slack *was* careful now: his movement had made him aware of something else. The boom of the shot had brought forth spectators. They stood at each corner of the hacienda, about a dozen of them all told. They had come silently, the way Verez's people usually did. They were grinning at the Indian youth's merriment. But they looked dangerous too.

'Help me to carry Jack,' said the big man and Piute Joe followed him over to the fallen one. Matu grinned at them and carried their hardware up on to the veranda to lay it at the master's feet.

Slack McGee said, 'We shall need them guns.'

'If you behave yourselves you can collect them on your way out,' said Verez.

With their burden the two men disappeared around a corner in the direction of the stores. Verez looked to the right and the left of him and made a motion with his hands. The spectators vanished. Only the attentive Matu still hovered near.

'Have you seen Pablo?' asked the old Mexican.

'No, *señor.*'

'Find him. Bring him here – sober, if possible.'

Matu made a little bow and loped away.

Pablo was Verez's *segunda.* He was not quite as old as his boss but almost as ornery. Three things he loved: fighting, tequila and Manuel Verez; maybe Verez should have come first on the list. If action promised Pablo could sober up in a second, no matter how much tequila he had imbibed. Verez kept him active as much as possible: he didn't want his *segunda* to drink himself into a premature grave: a man should live until ripeness and die with his boots on. Maybe, next to Matu, Verez loved Pablo most, although he upbraided him at every opportunity:

one had to make Pablo hard when the tequila soft-
ened him, for when hard he was the most cunning
and ruthless fighting man on the Rio Grande.

Pablo put in a quick appearance with Matu. He
said he had heard of the furore at the hacienda and
had been on his way. He wished to cut Slack McGee's
ears off and pin Piute Joe out for the jackals. Verez
said he had a better idea and he called his old friend
to sit beside him. He detected the fact that Pablo had
been in a bar when the news had reached him – but
very few other folks would have been aware of the
fact.

Verez leaned forward a little. 'This McGee has
government gold, *el patrio*, the fruits of the badly-
managed stage job we talked of – remember?'

Pablo tapped his forehead. 'Ah – now I remember.'

'It is not well that McGee should keep so much
money – particularly after he has made so much
grief.'

'It is not. We would have taken the money a neater
way.'

'But this way we do not want it.'

'No. I spit at the thought.' Pablo spat on the
veranda, then glanced nervously over his shoulder to
where Matu curled his lips at such sacrilege.

'However,' said Verez. 'Maybe it would be good if
we could we get the money and rid this place of the
pestilent McGee too. That man is getting too big for
his sombrero. Besides, could we not claim a reward
from the American government for the recovery of
stolen gold?'

A slow smile spread over Pablo's razor-sharp brown face. He slapped a thin knee. 'The US government paying money willingly to Manuel Verez! Ah, but that is rich!' He began to rise. 'I will see that the three men are killed right away. But yes – I will kill McGee myself.'

'Wait.' Verez laid a cautionary hand on his whip-like *segunda*'s arm. 'I do not wish that a mess should be made here in the settlement. We will let them go then you and I will ride after them.'

This pleased Pablo even more. 'My friend – but this will be like old times. We have not seen any action since the last time The Wolf visited us.'

'Ah, The Wolf,' said Verez. 'Now, there is a fighting man, a savage beast in human form. I wonder what has happened to him. How long is it since the last time we saw him?'

'Not too long,' said Pablo. 'Two – three months.'

'He was shot. Maybe he is dead.'

'Ah, but you do not believe that, *el patrio*. You would have to shoot The Wolf through the head like his namesake in order to kill him. Probably it is just that he is taking a little longer this time to lick his wounds. He lost quite a few men in the last little shindig. Probably he is recruiting more. He will be back.'

'Yes, he will be back.'

For a moment, Pablo thought he detected a note of weariness in his old friend's voice. But it was gone in a flash – as if it had not been there at all – and Pablo figured the drink must have been making him imagine things.

True, The Wolf had been a thorn in Manuel's side for the last couple of years or so. Rather a welcome thorn, as far as Pablo had been concerned, for the fighting men, since Manuel had seemed disinclined to ride far in his old age, had been getting soft. Then The Wolf had arrived and there had been hectic nights of strife, breakneck rides, and singing lead which had made Pablo's wicked heart sing with it.

Where the self-styled Wolf came from nobody knew. Some who had seen him in his gaudy raiment had said he was half-Indian. Legends grew around his name until it was almost as well-known along the border as was that of Verez. The young wolf to supplant the old. Little wonder that people said The Wolf coveted the settlement in order to rule the territory as king the way Verez had ruled these many years.

Well, The Wolf, that dirty half-caste ignorant bandido had tried to take the settlement more than once. And he had not succeeded yet. Pablo grinned; drew his gun with a speed that defied description.

Matu backed into the house. One must take care with such a madman, a man who spat on clean boards and brandished a gun like a liquored-up Injun with a scalping knife.

'Control yourself, my friend,' said Verez, and, a little sheepishly, Pablo put his gun away again.

'We will partake of a little food and drink and we will wait,' said Verez. He called Matu, gave him orders. The Indian youth left, to reappear a few moments later with a loaded tray on which reposed a daintily-garnished salad, a Jug of iced julep, glasses, plates and utensils. Pablo wrinkled his nose but made no comment. Evidently Manuel was making sure that his old comrade would be completely sober when the time came to ride.

'Help yourself, my friend,' said Manuel.

Pablo did as he was told. The sun began to dip, throwing bronze shadows across the veranda floor.

It was dusk when Slack McGee, Piute Joe and the wounded Jack returned for their guns.

'Jack ain't fit to ride,' said McGee.

'You ain't leaving me here with these buzzards,' said Jack.

McGee did not seem to hear him; went on, 'Jack ain't been the same since he had one lung punctured by a bullet a couple of years ago.'

Verez did not extend an invitation to Jack to stay and recuperate at the hacienda. In fact, the old Mexican did not say anything at all.

Jack burst out again querulously, 'You ain't leaving me. You ain't shaking me off like you did the others.'

'Shut your trap,' snarled McGee and made a threatening movement. Then he realized that Matu was standing like a shadow in the doorway. There was a faint shine from the barrel of the inevitable shotgun.

'I want no brawling on my veranda,' said Verez. 'Take your weapons and go, all three of you.'

The three men cautiously draped their weapons about them, Jack a little awkwardly because he had his arm in a sling and one shoulder looked twice as big as the other. They went down the veranda steps and on to their horses and mounted and rode till the dusk swallowed them up.

'Mebbe the jackals will fight among themselves,' said Pablo. 'And that will make our job easier.'

'We will get ready,' said Verez, and rose to his feet.

CHAPTER IX

Biddy was now riding with Pecos Charlie. The bluff old law-man seemed to have taken an enormous liking to the girl. Cal had been riding beside the old tracker, Nevada, in the forefront of the cavalcade but now he fell back and joined Brutus Calhoun at the back. Speaking so low that the others could not hear him he said:

'Brute, I'd like you to do something for me.'

'What's that, son?'

'Teach me to shoot straight – and fast.'

'That is rather a strange request.'

'Is it? I don't think so. Mebbe we wouldn't be searching the way we are now, if I could draw faster and shoot straighter . . .'

'You're a rancher, Cal – a man of peace.'

'No longer,' said Cal. 'Besides, a man of peace often has to become a man of action in order to defend that peace.'

'I ride beside you and my function is not as a preacher anymore, but as a fighting man,' said Brute, a little sadly. 'Therefore I would not be justified in arguing with you . . .'

Cal pressed home his advantage: 'If I had been faster on the draw and a straight shooter that first jasper wouldn't have gotten away from me in San Antone. He was a professional killer an' I was like an unlicked babe – it was a wonder he didn't put paid to me altogether. At the station I was too slow as well – I might have plugged either Slack McGee or his pard. I get my dander up quickly, but I haven't got the cold-blooded speed, both in mind and in movement, that is needed . . .'

Cal's voice died away, then spurted again. Now it was almost as if he was talking only to himself. 'Fin's life was thrown away. He rode with me because I was his friend. If I had been a gunfighter mebbe I would've been able to save his life . . . I dunno . . .'

'We all have thoughts of that kind,' said Brute. 'I do myself. I think I should've saved Fin. I *was* a gunfighter remember?' The big man's voice had a bitter ring.

'I'm sorry, Brute, I didn't realize,' Cal was quickly contrite. 'Hell, all I seem to be thinking of lately is myself and what has happened to me – what has happened to Lucinda. You're doing a lot for me – taking up your guns again . . .'

'I'm doing it for all of us – for the town,' Brute swung out a hand in one of the magnificent gestures he used when preaching. 'For all this – it will be a cleaner place when such people as Slack McGee are wiped from the face of it. Mebbe I have been burying my head in the sand too much of late, Cal, or walking with my head in the clouds. A man must look about him now and then, must be prepared to fight if need be. Mebbe in a way I needed this . . .'

'Then you'll teach me your tricks, Brute?'

'Yes, I'll teach you. If you will promise to hang up your guns again as soon as your task is finished. The life of a gunfighter is a terrible one and can only have one end. I have been lucky – but I can name dozens of my ilk who haven't. Will you promise?'

'I'll promise,' said Cal softly.

'Lights,' called Nevada suddenly.

'That must be the Verez settlement,' said Brute. 'So it's still there.'

'So soon,' said Cal. 'Mebbe I won't get a chance to have the first lesson, oldtimer.' He rubbed his calloused hands together. He had worked hard back at the ranch, getting it ready for Lucinda. There was no smoothness in those joints and finger-tips, no suppleness in those wrists. He rubbed one hand down the smooth neck of his horse.

Brutus Calhoun said, 'Don't worry. You'll get by.'

About half-an-hour later they rode into the settlement. Dark-skinned men, most of them armed to the teeth, eyed the newcomers cautiously. They draped their reins over the hitch-rail and entered the lighted cantina.

A lean, middle-aged, hard-faced Mex came forward. He had only one arm, and a permanent smoulder in his dark eyes.

'Hullo, Joaquin,' said Brutus Calhoun.

The man's eyes sparked with suspicion. He peered nearer, then began to smile, though the smile did not reach the sad and savage eyes.

'Señor Calhoun.'

'None other, Joaquin. How are you?'

The Mexican gave an eloquent little shrug. 'As always. But I hear strange things about you, *amigo.*'

'The strange things are true, Joaquin.'

'But now you wear your guns again.'

Brute smiled thinly behind his walrus moustache. 'There is a job I have to do – my friends and I – afterwards I will hang up my guns and those strange things will come over me again. Where is Manuel, Joaquin?'

'Out riding.'

'And Pablo?'

'They are riding together.'

'As in the old days,' said Brutus softly. 'Could we have hot food and drink in a hurry, Joaquin?'

'Yes.' The one-armed Mexican bobbed and disappeared behind his counter.

'Why didn't you ask him?' hissed Cal.

'I intend to. But you can't rush these people. Many of them are outlaws themselves, you know. The three men we want may be hiding here.'

And now, as they sat down, Cal became aware of the tension, of the silence in the cantina, although it was fairly full of people. He looked around him. Dark eyes were turned away from him as he did so. A buzz of talk suddenly broke out again; crockery rattled. For a time, it seemed, Joaquin had accepted these strangers. The assembly was prepared to do this also – but, if they proved to be enemies, a score of knives would leap to their throats at a word.

Joaquin returned, behind him an Indian boy bearing a groaning tray, which he placed on the table. The one-armed man then waved him away and bent to place out the food himself.

'We are looking for three men,' said Brute softly. 'The leader a big man with a scar.'

'The McGee,' said Joaquin jubilantly out of the corner of his mouth. 'You want his scalp?'

'We do.'

Joaquin turned away from the table to spit, a mere gesture. 'He is a pig. We turned him away from here at sundown. He and his two friends. One was wounded. He argued with Manuel and Manuel's Indian boy shot him.'

'Matu? He is grown up now, huh?'

'Yes, Matu is grown up – and he shoots straight.'

'Manuel and Pablo have gone out after the three men maybe?' whispered Brute.

Joaquin shrugged. 'Who knows? They do not tell me these things.' He moved away.

'That is all we'll get from him,' said Brutus. 'Later we'll tackle the Indian boy. Let's eat. I guess we need some warm sustenance.'

Cal was the first to push away his half-empty plate. 'I've had enough. I'll go and see to the horses.'

'I'll come and help you,' said Biddy.

They unhitched the horses and led them to the 'dobe building which housed the stables. There a fat Mexican promised to rub down, water and feed the beasts for them. Cal asked him about the three men, their leader, a big man with a scar. The fat hostler shrugged his shoulders, shook his head until it was in danger of coming off.

Cal gave up. Outside he said, 'Well, my spot of detective work wasn't very clever was it?'

The girl smiled. 'We can only keep on trying.'

She reflected that he seemed to have thrown off his gloom. She was glad of this, but could understand how he had felt. She had lost a loved one too. She wondered what kind of a woman his bride had been. Beautiful probably; but the kind of wilting city type that these rugged plainsmen often fell for. But maybe she was being unfair to him and to the memory of a dead girl . . . She had to trot a little in order to keep up with his long strides. He slowed down, said he was sorry.

'You're raring to go, aren't you?' she said, using the old Western lingo she had picked up in the gambling-halls.

'Guess I am,' he admitted. 'Are you?'

'I suppose so.'

'I admire your guts,' he blurted out. Then shut his mouth tightly as if sorry he had spoken.

There was no time for further conversation. They had reached the cantina and the rest of the bunch were already out on the veranda awaiting them.

Brutus Calhoun led the way.

The hacienda was in darkness, but they skirted it and saw a lighted window at the back. The veranda went all around the place. They climbed into it and Brutus knocked on the back door. It was flung open and the muzzle of a shotgun was poked into the big man's belly.

'Take it easy, Matu,' said the big man.

The hard muzzle was lowered a little. Like Joaquin had done, Matu peered into the tall man's face, breathed his name. He, too, had heard rumours about the fabulous Calhoun and his strange doings. But 'the master' had many friends whose ways were strange and changeable . . . and Matu remembered the swashbuckling Brutus of old. He asked the moustached man and his friends into the house and all the time Brutus was talking fast.

Matu seemed a little puzzled by the presence of a girl. But finally he admitted that Pablo and the master had gone after Slack McGee, Piute Joe and the wounded man called Jack.

'Let's go,' said Cal Mackey.

Matu waved aside the silver dollar Brutus offered him. 'Go with God,' he said simply.

'Thank you, my son,' said Brutus. Then he grinned and punched the Indian affectionately on the shoulder with clenched fist, the way he used to do when Matu was a shaver, hero-worshipping the tall, dark gunman with the laughing eyes.

Matu grinned back; he stood at the doorway and watched them go, waved before they disappeared into the dusk.

They were all tired but, hoping now that their chase was near its end, wanted to get to the other side of the river before resting. They reached the ferry, the huge raft, and paid the fees for their horses and themselves to be poled across by the fat, burly Mexican with one eye.

Cal said, 'Did you see . . .' Then broke off, as Brutus caught his arm in a grip that made him wince.

The wind had arisen and blustered at them. The Rio was rough, the horses restive. It was not until, with sighs of relief, the party reached the opposite bank that Brutus had a chance to explain his action.

'You would've got nothing from the ferryman, believe me, Cal. Asking about Verez or the other men would only have awakened his suspicions. He might've got half the settlement on our heels. We don't want that, do we?'

'I guess not,' said Cal ruefully. He managed to grin. 'I guess the best thing I can do is keep my big mouth shut.'

'That ferryman's watching us,' said Pecos Charlie out of the corner of his mouth. 'Let's move on a leetle.'

They went on into the dusk. When they looked back again, the ferryman had vanished, had doubtless taken his raft back to its moorings.

A jumble of rocks, the edge of the strip of badlands which separated the river from the more fertile country further inland, began to swallow up the riders.

'The lamp,' said Nevada. 'I guess it's safe to light it now.'

He took it, lit it, dismounting at the same time. He went on ahead but returned fairly promptly.

'A whole mess o' tracks,' he said. 'I picked out the marks o' that unshod horse again – Piute Joe's, I guess. Seems like McGee and his friends weren't taking much care. I guess they didn't figure anybody would follow 'em.

'Why would Verez follow 'em?' said Cal.

It was Brutus who answered. 'Who can tell with Verez? Mebbe he wants the Government gold. Mebbe he just wants McGee's scalp. Whichever it is, you can be sure he holds an ace card somewhere. He wouldn't hit the trail again at his age unless somethin' was prickling him.'

'D'you think he'd take a chance on the Government money?' asked Pecos Charlie.

'Not if he knew how it had been got.'

Nevada had doused the lantern. Now he remounted and led the way.

The old man halted again so suddenly that the marshal's horse almost ran into him.

Nevada's horse had been startled by the sudden jerk on the reins. The beast reared. 'Look out!' yelled Nevada. 'There's . . .'

The rest of his words were drowned by a hideous blatter of gunfire, tearing the night to shreds. Tongues of flame blossomed from the rocks to the right of the party. Nevada fell backwards over his horse's tail, hit the ground almost under the hoofs of the marshal's mount.

CHAPTER X

'Take cover,' yelled Pecos Charlie. He slid from the
saddle, moving surprisingly fast on his peg-leg,
grabbed Nevada under the armpits and dragged him
clear of flailing hoofs.

The night was hideous with gunfire. There was the
sickening sound of a bullet striking flesh. Charlie's
horse gave a shrill scream of agony and crumpled up.

To Cal Mackey things seemed to happen like
something in a confused speeded-up nightmare.
Brute Calhoun had drawn his gun with almost unbe-
lievable rapidity, was wheeling his horse to cover
Biddy as he sent shots winging into the darkness. In
the gun-flash Cal caught sight of his friend's face. It
was a set mask, the teeth revealed whitely beneath
the handsome moustache, the eyes mere slits.

Brute waved his free hand, began to yank at his
horse's reins. The small party began to move back to
the cover of the rocks behind them. Cal caught hold
of the bridle of Biddy's horse. In his other hand he
held his gun, though he had no recollection of
having drawn it. As they backed together, their

84

horses' shoulders almost touching, he saw that Biddy had a gun in her hand too. They reached the cover of the rocks, dismounting as they did so. They were thrown together by the turmoil of their startled horses. Cal caught hold of the girl to steady her. He felt the firm softness of her body against his and was unaccountably touched.

'Down,' she said urgently. As he sank beside her in cover, a slug whisked his hat off.

Brutus was bringing up the rear, man and beast huge against the night sky. Brutus, an avenging figure with flaming weapons. There was a lull in the shooting from the hidden bushwhackers. Biddy and Cal sighed with relief as they saw the big man and his horse get into cover a little way away from them. After that their anxiety was for old Nevada and they crawled towards where he lay with Marshal Heckerstein.

The latter said, 'They got him in the thigh.'

'Just a flea-bite,' said Nevada.

'Flea-bite hell!' snarled Charlie. 'You're bleeding like a stuck pig. Hold still, you consarned ol' skunk!'

Now Brutus ran half-stooping along the rocks to them. The hidden marksman saw his movement and tried to pick him off but failed to do so. As soon as Brute had satisfied himself that his old pard was alive, as well as kicking, he sent a barrage back at the dark shapes of the rocks. Cal joined him, while Biddy and Charlie, using the tail of the latter's shirt, bound Nevada's wound.

'No more riding for you a while, oldtimer,' said Pecos Charlie.

Nevada snorted. Out of respect for Miss Biddy he did not curse, but he sounded as if he wanted to. 'How the heck am I gonna get my hands on them skunks if I don't ride?'

Brutus Calhoun turned his head. 'You don't have to ride to get at them, Nevada. All you've got to do is walk a few hundred yards . . .'

'An' get yourself filled full o' lead,' concluded Cal Mackey for him.

'The ol' mossy-horn ain't gonna find it very easy to walk for some time either,' said Charlie. 'Mebbe that's as well anyway, the plumb foolish way he's acting right now.'

'Where's my gun then?' demanded Nevada, wrathfully. 'Just gimme my gun.'

'You must've dropped it!'

There was a lull in the shooting. Cal said to Brutus, 'D'yuh really think it's Slack McGee an' his pards over there?'

'Who else could it be?'

'It could be your pal, Verez.'

'I don't think he would shoot from ambush,' said Brutus; adding wryly, 'Leastways until he was perfectly sure who he was shooting at.'

'Mebbe he mistook us for the Slack McGee party.'

'Then he can't count. . . ! I'll soon find out anyway.'

Brutus raised his voice. 'That you, Manuel, you old buzzard? This is Brute Calhoun.'

'No, it ain't your pal, Verez,' replied a jeering voice. This was followed by a barrage of shots, making the defenders duck their heads. 'That's Slack

McGee all right,' said Pecos Charlie grimly.

The firing died down again. Cal and Brutus ceased to retaliate. Cal said, 'I wonder what happened to Verez and his pard.'

'I was wondering that myself,' said Brutus in a worried voice. 'I hope the skunks haven't bush-whacked them, left them lying someplace.'

'If they had, why would they be hanging around here. They couldn't have known we were on their tails. Surely they would've gotten away from here as fast as they could in case there were more of the Mexican band after them.'

'I hope you're right. Maybe they threw Verez off the trail, then doubled back. That'd be quite a trick: Verez is no mean tracker.'

'Maybe they've already been ambushed. Maybe they're lying out there somewhere. Do you think the shooting will be heard the other side of the river?'

'I doubt it,' said Brutus. 'The wind's blowing in the other direction and it's kinda blustery too . . .'

'There goes somebody,' cried Cal. But Brutus had already seen the moving shape and his gun bucked and flamed.

There was no more movement then, but they could not be sure whether Brute had hit anybody. Shooting was pretty desultory on both sides. Both parties were well-covered now.

Nevada's doctoring was finished and the old mossy-horn had been given a spare gun. Now he, together with Biddy and Pecos Charlie, joined Brutus and Cal behind their barricade. The girl was told to get back, keep low, but paid no attention. She held her gun, a business-like .32, purposefully, and was as grim-looking as her male companions.

She wriggled her way in between Brutus and Cal; for a moment a strand of her hair blew across the latter's face. He opened his mouth to tell her to take care, but the words were taken away from him by a hideous blatter of shooting from the other side. He saw her lift the gun. It flamed; her face was set in the fitful orange light but it was, somehow, very beautiful too. Momentarily, as the flash blossomed and died, Cal was reminded poignantly of another lovely face . . .

Then rock particles stung his cheek from a ricocheted bullet and he fired at the flashes opposite. The night was once more like a nightmare. Booming guns, hectic flashes, the stink of cordite, smoke that stung the throat and eyes. He looked at Biddy again to ascertain that she was still all right. He realized she knew how a handle a gun, was a good shot; maybe a better shot than he was himself.

On the other side of him, Brutus was triggering his gun like a well-oiled machine. In the quieter intervals he could hear Nevada chortling. The old man's leg was surely paining him; but that didn't seem to be cramping his style none.

Very little could be seen of the other side. The defenders fired at movements, shadows, flashes. Cal realized that could go on almost indefinitely. He hissed to Brutus, 'I'm going to see if I can get around behind them. Pass the word along. Keep 'em busy – keep me covered.'

Brutus nodded. Cal backed, began to crawl. Biddy

turned. Her lips formed the words: 'Where are you going?'

He made a half-circular movement with his hand. She began to crawl after him but Brutus grabbed her, pulled her back, and finally she desisted.

Cal went on a bit further under cover of the rocks, then paused. He realized he would have to cross a flat empty space in order to get near the outcrop behind which the outlaws lurked. His friends were sending across a blistering fire, pinning the outlaws down. Gun in hand, Cal tensed himself. Then, half-stooping, he began to run. A slug buzzed past his head and he knew that they had spotted him, that his manoeuvre had failed. Pieces of rock spurted into his face; he winced as they bit into his flesh, then he rolled into the cover of a small boulder.

The cover was inadequate. Bullets were seeking him out. One took a chunk of leather from the heel of his boot; another almost singed his breeches. He knew he had to move – and quick! – if he wanted to stay all in one piece. The thought was father to the action. He scuttled like a jack-rabbit. Another slug plucked at his shirt at the back. Then he was rolling in cover, cutting himself to pieces on biting shale . . .

He rose on one knee, surprised to find that his gun was still in his hand. Things happened now, confused, at lightning speed. A figure loomed up before him. He felt the hot breath of a slug past his face. He fired from the hip, his lips drawn back from his teeth, his eyes squinted against the smoke and the dust. He heard a scream and the dark figure was foreshortened before him and he felt wild, savage exultation. He hadn't missed this time!

The figure was crumpled now, shapeless, still. But (Cal blinked his smoke-filled eyes) another was rising in its place. He tilted the gun a little, mechanically, pressed the trigger. The report was deafening and he knew that he had missed, that the other man was firing too, the echoes rolling. Something smote him on the head, a huge fireball exploded in his brain, in a myriad of fiery particles. Then he was falling . . . falling, in abyssal blackness . . .

He could hear voices and he struggled up through layers of woolly darkness to reach them. Finally it seemed that something was trying to help him and, after that, things were not so hard. There was a roaring in his ears and he felt giddy, but he was still alive. Somebody's arm was around his shoulders, lifting him. A voice said, 'He's coming to. Just a nasty crease, I guess.'

The voice enlivened him. He recognized it as Brute Calhoun's. He realized he was safe. Was the battle over? What was he lying here for?

He struggled upwards. The grip tightened around his shoulders. 'Take it easy, oldtimer,' said Brutus.

It was still darkness, but a darkness comparatively light after the blackness into which he had been plunged. Faces began to form around him. The faces of all his friends, all alive. Biddy looked at him anxiously and moved nearer . . .

'Let me take a look at that head,' she said.

He felt her cool fingers touch his temple and he

lay back across Brute's arm. 'What happened to Slack McGee?' he croaked.

'Never mind about him,' replied the big man, almost brusquely.

Cal, trying to think of another pertinent question, winced as Biddy's once-gentle fingers probed the wound.

'Sorry,' said the girl; then, on an aside, 'It's a nasty gash. It needs some stitches in it – or some good doctoring anyway. Can't do much here.'

'The same goes for Nevada,' said Pecos Charlie. 'We better get 'em both back to the settlement.'

'How about McGee. . . ?'

'He got away,' said Marshal Heckerstein. 'So, as far as we can make out, did his wounded friend Jack. You got Piute Joe, plugged him right between the eyes. You took a chance, younker, a mighty big chance. You gave us a chance too – to rush them. But they got on their horses and lit out.'

'Why didn't you get after them?'

'And leave you here to die? In any case, our horses weren't at hand. Them two jaspers got a big start.'

Cal realized he had been ungracious. 'Sorry,' he mumbled. His head felt like a mule was stomping on it. His commonsense reasserted itself. He realized he could not possibly ride in this condition. At least he had got one of the skunks – though it was a pity it hadn't been McGee, or even Jack, instead of their catspaw.

Biddy produced a cloth from somewhere and bound up his head. 'The blood's caked,' she said. 'That will hold it for a while – unless it bursts open again.'

The horses were brought forward and Cal allowed himself to be helped on to his own mount. They had a little trouble with Nevada. Before anybody could stop him he had tried to climb on to his own horse. His wounded leg gave way beneath him and he collapsed. They left Cal in order to help the pig-headed old mossy back. Cal held on like grim death, the world spinning around him. He felt a hand on his arm and turned to look into the face of Biddy. She smiled at him, giving him confidence.

Finally the cantankerous Nevada was upright in the saddle. The party set off back the way they had come. The breeze began to clear Cal's head a little. Biddy rode on one side of him, Brute on the other. They were very close: he realized they were ready to catch him if he began to sway. He told himself grimly that he was going to ride the way he always rode. What he had got was only a flea-bite – he had a vague idea he'd heard that description somewhere before – he was going back to the settlement to get fixed up some-how, then he was going out again after Slack McGee, even if he had to go alone, even if he had to chase the coyote plumb to the other side of Mexico . . .

His mind flitted around as if something had been knocked haywire by the blow to his head. He turned suddenly to Brute and said, 'Did you find Verez or his pard?'

'Not a smell of 'em,' said the big man. 'The ground might've opened and swallowed 'em up.'

The river reached, Pecos Charlie gave a shout and tugged at the guide-rope which led across to the ferrylanding. After a few moments, and another couple of hails, the raft, with its fat custodian, hove into sight from the darkness.

'We've got a couple of wounded men here,' said the marshal. 'We must get 'em back to the settlement.'

'How did they get wounded?' asked the burly Mexican gutturally.

'We had a brush with that scarfaced skunk McGee an' his two pards.'

The Mex's face was inscrutable in the half-light. 'Where is Verez?' he asked.

'We don't know. We wish we did.'

The Mexican was suspicious. How did he know it was not Verez with whom these strange gringoes had had a shooting affray? He was either a very brave man or a very foolish one. He went for his gun.

Pecos Charlie's own weapon cleared leather a split second before. The Mexican, his gun half out of its holster, looked death in the face. 'Lift it out gently an' drop it,' said the marshal gently.

The man did as he was told.

'Now pole us to the other side – an' no tricks.'

The fat greaser turned sullenly to his task. The waves lapped over the edge of the raft. The opposite shore hove in sight.

'Take it gently – gently,' said Pecos Charlie. His gunbarrel prodded gently but ominously into the man's back.

The ferryman growled something uncomplimentary in bastardised Spanish but, with the skill of long practice, brought the raft around neatly. It grated gently on the shingle.

The fat man's next move was totally unexpected. He jumped suddenly in the air, brought down all his weight on the edge of the raft so that it rocked violently, throwing the rest of its occupants off-balance as they were already moving to disembark. Biddy would have fallen overboard had not Cal grabbed her around the waist. The wounded Nevada rolled to the edge of the raft and clung on grimly while the waves lapped coldly over his lean body. Brute Calhoun bent, grabbed the lean body, held on to it. Pecos Charlie teetered crazily, his gun pointed skywards. He righted himself, pointed the gun at the fat shadow fleeing into the darkness. Then he lowered the gun, moving forward at the same time. A shot would bring the whole settlement about their ears, and that was the last thing they wanted.

He moved at a surprising rate, his peg-leg making a frantic thumping sound. But the Mexican was no sloth himself and soon disappeared in a clump of trees. Throwing caution over his shoulder, the marshal dived in after him. He half-admired the fat fool, a brave fat fool. He had not even yelled for help. Maybe he wanted to handle things all by himself or maybe he figured that once he raised an outcry the shooting might begin and, unarmed, he might get in the way of some hot lead.

Crashing through the trees, his gun held purposefully, Charlie was pretty sure he would catch up with the fat freak.

The latter evidently had the same idea, for he suddenly materialized from the darkness, from the cover of a tree behind which he had been lurking.

Something flashed dully in his uplifted hand, something which in that split moment of revelation,
Charlie wished he had looked for when he had taken
the greaser's gun. Didn't they all carry a knife,
shouldn't he know enough about them by now. . . ?

But no more thought now, only action. He
swerved, ducked, flinching away from the blow. It
missed him: he could imagine he heard the whistle
of the cold steel. The Mexican had been too hasty.
The force of the blow jerked his bulk off balance.
The marshal, teetering on his good leg, brought the
other one round in a sweeping half-circle. The peg-
leg cracked against the fat man's shin and, involuntarily, he howled with pain. He fell on his face.
Charlie bent, swung the gun. It landed with a dull
crump and the fat bulk quivered once more, then
became still.

Pecos Charlie straightened up, his head cocked on
one side. He hoped the greaser's yell had not been
heard. There were thudding footsteps, but they
seemed to be coming from the direction of the river.
They ceased suddenly as if the man had stopped to
listen. The marshal bent once more over the prone
form at his feet and made sure that the ferryman was
going to sleep for quite a while. Then he began to
move slowly back the way he had come, not even his
peg-leg making a sound on the soft ground now.

On the edge of the trees he came suddenly upon
the other man and raised his gun. Steel glinted in
front of him and he called harshly, frantically, 'Hold
it.'

The other figure became immobile, the steel hung

uselessly, the white bandage shone on the tousled head.

'Marshal,' cried Cal Mackey.

'Gosh, I almost blew a hole in you,' said Pecos Charlie.

'We almost blew a hole in each other,' said Cal, a little shakily. 'Did you catch that fat skunk?'

'Yeh. Where are the others?'

'They're all right. They're coming on along.'

'The fat Mex is unconscious back there. Give me a hand to truss him up with something before he comes round.'

'I better dodge back an' warn the others first.' Cal's bandaged head wagged a little.

'Take care o' that haid,' said the marshal.

'I'm all right,' was the curt reply.

'Right.'

Cal turned, disappeared into the darkness and, in a few moments, came trotting back.

The two men trussed the unconscious ferryman up with his own gunbelt and his fancy sash. They gagged him with his own 'kerchief and rolled him into a hole in the under brush. Then they joined the others at the edge of the trees.

'Make a detour to the house,' said Brute Calhoun, leading the way.

CHAPTER XI

Again they were met at the back door by Matu with his shotgun. The Indian youth asked the same question as the ferryman had asked but was not so suspicious after Brutus had told the story.

Nevada, cursing with unwonted mildness because of the presence of the girl, was helped on to a couch in the huge stone-walled kitchen. Cal Mackey let himself fall into a commodious rocking chair. His exertions with Marshal Heckerstein and the unconscious ferryman had taken more out of him than he had thought. His head felt like it was split in half, and the room was becoming a shimmering blur. Biddy bent over him. He could smell the fragrance of her hair. She patted his hand.

'How are you feeling?'

'I'm all right, thanks.' With an effort he straightened himself up, tried to get things in focus.

Her dark eyes were looking into his, he knew that much. She said: 'You don't look too good. Lean back.'

She rested her hands on his shoulders and he let himself be pushed gently back into the chair. 'I'll go and fix Nevada up then come back and take a look at that head,' she said and moved away.

Things were back in focus again now and he tilted his head to watch her cross the room. Despite the mannish riding habit she looked all woman. Her figure was superb. She was lithe and healthy-looking. She looked as if she had been born on the untamed, elemental frontier. She was a sight to fire a strong man's blood.

Cal felt a warm tide begin to envelop his face, make his head pulse alarmingly again. He turned his head away, let it fall back on the hard chair so that pain shot through it. It was as if he was punishing himself for his disloyalty to the dead Lucinda.

Matu, reared in an atmosphere of strife and quite familiar with gunshot wounds, moved with quiet efficiency. He boiled water, found bandages and salve. Nevada kept up a running stream of badinage as Biddy got to work on him. The oldtimer was in considerable pain, but an ignorant listener might have thought he was listening-in to the ranch humorist at the annual barbecue.

Brutus Calhoun joined Cal, answered the young man's question. The bullet had not, fortunately, lodged in Nevada's leathery thigh, but ploughed itself through and out on a sidelong course.

'Good job, too,' went on the big ex-preacher reflectively. 'Or he would've needed a doctor mebbe. We got to figure what to do next – an' quick.'

'Leave Nevada here an' get after those skunks,' said Cal vehemently.

'Yes, and have you fall off your horse.'

'I'm all right.' Cal was sweating. He gripped the arms of the chair.

'Oh, sure – sure,' growled Brutus.

'What's going on here?' carolled the voice of Marshal Heckerstein, and Cal realized that Nevada was finished with and it was his turn.

'He's all right,' said Brutus sardonically. 'He aims to tuck his head under his arm and go out after Slack McGee right now.'

'The pore young coot's delirious,' sang out Nevada from the other side of the room.

Cal jerked upwards. 'I could stand on my haid a whole lot quicker than you could stand on that pesky leg of yourn, you old crowbait,' he yelled back.

His head began to spin and he involuntarily let himself fall back into the chair again.

'Young or old, they're all alike,' said Biddy. 'Pigheaded. Keep still.'

Cal allowed her to take away his improvised bandage. Her touch was cool and gentle as she bathed the shallow wound with warm water, spread it with salve and made a more workmanlike job of it with clean fresh bandaging.

Matu had returned again with mugs of hot coffee laced with whiskey and a stack of buckwheat biscuits. Cal allowed himself to have food and drink forced on him. The throbbing in his head had quietened now and a delicious latitude began to steal over his limbs. He tried to fight it off but did not succeed. He had been pushing himself too hard, he needed rest badly . . .

He awoke suddenly – when the kitchen door crashed open. Mechanically, he groped for his gun, then realized it was not there. The lighted kitchen, huge though it was, suddenly seemed overfull of people. He recognized the fat ferryman instantly and wondered who had let him free. Maybe he had got himself loose: he had been as slippery as an eel. Cal did not like the look of the wicked Frontier model Colt the fat frog held in his podgy fist.

He was not the only one with a levelled gun either. Joaquin, the one-armed storeman, had one too, and so had the other dozen or so Mexicans grouped around him.

Brutus and the rest of the boys had been taken completely by surprise and now a Mexican was going amongst them relieving them of their hardware. He leered at Biddy as he touched her. She slapped his face, the sound like a pistol-shot in the stillness. He staggered back, then reached for her again, swearing gutterally.

'That's enough!' rapped Joaquin.

The offender jumped as if he had been shot. Though he might only be a one-armed storekeeper, Joaquin evidently carried some weight with this bunch. He was obviously in an even more wicked temper than usual.

The guns were dropped at his feet. Across them he eyed Brutus Calhoun.

'Where is Manuel?' he asked.

100

Brute told his story once more, the same story he had told the ferryman and Matu.

Joaquin listened silently until the tale was finished, then jerked a thumb and asked silkily, 'Then why did you attack him?'

The ferryman shifted his feet and glowered. Pecos Charlie put in, 'I was the one who slugged him. He pulled a gun on us.'

'He did not believe your story,' said Joaquin. 'Is not that understandable?'

'Is it?' said Brutus. 'Is it that you doubt our word, too, Joaquin? That you doubt *my* word?'

'I used to know Brutus,' said Joaquin. 'The Brutus I see now has changed.' He shrugged his shoulders. 'Who knows?'

'So, because a fat ignorant pig does not believe anything you do not believe it either.'

The ferryman growled deep in his throat and started forward. Joaquin halted him with a gesture.

'If it is all true, this you say, Brutus, is it not strange that Manuel and Pablo have not returned yet?'

'It is strange,' agreed Brutus.

Joaquin turned his case to Matu, standing impassively in a corner.

'Do you not think it is strange, small Indian, that the master has not yet returned?'

'I do.'

'Yet you take in these men, you believe their story?'

'Brutus is my old friend, my uncle, my blood-brother. He would not lie. He is the master's friend too, why should he kill him. . . ?'

'Why, yes. But Brutus now is not the Brutus we

101

knew. We have heard strange things about him, he has changed.'

'I do not think he has changed. He was always a good man.'

'A gunfighter, a good man!'

'Some good men walk alone. They walk alone because they *are* good. Things are forced upon them because they walk alone and worship no man.' The young Matu had learned much of Manuel Verez's philosophy and cunning, he was no dumb Indian.

'You talk in riddles,' Joaquin told him, with a thin smile. 'Do you ally yourselves with these people against us?'

'I do what I think the master would wish me to do.'

'You have swept floors too long, small Indian,' said Joaquin. 'You are an Indian with no guts.'

Matu's eyes smouldered but he made no movement. Those guns were too menacing. He had stoicism; but no tendency to suicide.

Joaquin's voice rang out harshly, 'I am not gutless. I do not believe everything I am told. I do not believe this man; this preacher who used to be my friend. I believe his preaching is a joke with which he fools simple men. I believe that he is on the owlhoot again – he and his friends. I believe he is after the Government gold which Slack McGee is supposed to have stolen.' He backed a little, turned his head slightly. 'What do you say out there?'

Another Mexican appeared in the doorway. 'There is nothing with the horses, Joaquin.'

'I did not think there would be. They would be

102

crazy to bring the stuff with them. It could be hidden.'

Brutus Calhoun spoke again now. 'I don't know what deep game you think you are playing, Joaquin. One of Slack McGee's friends lies dead the other side of the river. That body will prove that at least part of my story is true. You might even find a clue there.' The big man's voice was soft, almost gentle.

Joaquin's lips quirked in a mirthless smile. He came to a decision. 'Let us all go to the store – you also, Matu.'

The cavalcade moved out of the hacienda and across the yard and into a back room of the store, a smelly place packed high with old boxes and fragments of merchandise. Rope was produced and, surrounded by a battery of menacing guns, the prisoners had to submit to being placed in a sitting position on the floor and having their hands and feet tied. Great care was taken with the indignant Biddy. Joaquin evidently thought that what he was doing was right; but he was no brute, not with women, at least.

'Three of us will go and look for this dead man and these clues you speak of; Matu will come with us.'

'I'll watch this bunch,' said the fat ferryman.

Joaquin smiled his mirthless smile again. 'No, I think that would be unwise. I want them to be unharmed for when I return.' He surveyed the prisoners. 'It was very unwise of you to attack this man.'

'He attacked us first,' said Pecos Charlie, grinning.

The old marshal seemed utterly unperturbed by recent happenings.

Brutus said: 'We have two wounded men . . .'

'I'm all right,' put in Cal Mackey. 'All I want to do is get my hands around that one-armed skunk's neck.'

Joaquin's eyes sparked hotly and he started forward. Then he checked himself, the thin smile on his lean dark face once more. He told his men to place Nevada on an old, broken-down couch in a dark corner. He detailed four men to watch the prisoners, then the rest of them left.

Shadows crouched in the corners and angles where, separated from each other, the trussed people lay. On a small battered table beneath the single dusty light-bulb, the four Mexicans sat on packing cases and played cards. Money began to chink. The concentration became almost painful.

Cal Mackey surreptitiously struggled with his bonds, but all he succeeded in doing was making his wrists sore and aching. From where he sat, propped against an old box which smelt pungently of stale fish, he had a good view of the card-players but only a poor one of his companions. In fact, he could not see Brutus and Nevada at all and had only a glimpse of Pecos Charlie's peg-leg and the smooth lines of Biddy's profile in the half light.

'You feel all right, oldtimer?' said Brute's voice.

Nevada answered forcibly. He sounded like he was about to explode. 'Jest somebody let me loose an' I'll show you. I still got one good leg. Quite enough to stamp on rats.'

One of the Mexicans turned away from his game and guffawed loudly. One of his companions called him sharply to attention. 'Jose! What did you do with that card?'

Jose was fat and greasy with a dirty face that split from ear to ear when he grinned. His thick eyebrows rose, his eyes bugged with exaggerated astonishment. 'What card, *amigo*?'

'That was very funny,' said the other man. 'To turn around in the chair like that and bray like an ass when it was your turn to play.'

'I do not understand, amigo!'

'You do not!' The other's voice rose. He sprang from his chair and went around the table.

The greasy one rose involuntarily, then made a wild grab downwards. But the card fell from his lap to the floor. His accuser, tall and thin, towered over him, cuffed him on the side of the head, sending him staggering. He went for his gun. The tall Mex hit him again, low down. He grunted, doubled, fell on his side. His gun clattered on the floor, slid to within a few feet of Cal Mackey.

The fat man had a friend who stepped behind the lean one and slugged him with a gun-butt. The lean one joined the groaning fat one on the floor, but did not make a sound. Cal Mackey looked with terrible fascination at the gun and hoped nobody else had noticed it.

But by now the two Mexicans who remained on their feet were too busy arguing volubly.

Cal prayed that they would fight.

The fat greasy man climbed painfully to his feet,

saw his fallen foe and kicked him viciously in the ribs. This started the unconscious one's friend off: he ran at the fat one. In a second there was a regular free-for-all. Cal Mackey began to wriggle his way, on his rump, across the floor. He did not know whether he would be able to grab the gun when he got to it, but he was going to have a darned good try.

The lean man was coming to his senses. He joined the fray the quickest way he could: by grabbing somebody's ankles and pulling. It was his old enemy, the fat one, who fell, landing with a crash almost on top of Cal Mackey, landing on the back of his head and lying stunned. Cal twisted himself around, grabbed the fellow's knife.

The lean man looked at the prisoner suspiciously, but Cal already had the knife behind his back. The lean man opened his mouth to say something and received a sly fist in his ear. He whirled, teeth bared, as he reached for his own knife.

Cal sawed desperately at his bonds. He almost cried out with pain as he gashed his wrist. The warm, sticky blood bathed his flesh, made the ropes gummy, harder to cut. But he persevered and finally they parted, but the agony of returning circulation was far greater than the knife-wound had been.

Cal gritted his teeth, his wounded head began to spin around. He fought off nausea, trying to focus his attention on the fight while he massaged his wrists behind him. He was glad to discover that the knife-wound was a small one. Gradually his hands got back to normal again. He flexed the fingers.

He picked up the knife. He braced himself. Then,

as he grabbed for the gun, he tossed the knife with his other hand. He might not have been a gunfighter, but he was no slouch as a knife-thrower. The blade quivered in the boards a few inches from Brute Calhoun's side.

Cal straightened up. 'Hold it,' he said, harshly. 'Hold it, or I'll start shooting.'

The three men whirled, backed. One of them reached for his gun, then thought better of it.

'Up with your hands,' said the wild-looking young man.

The three Mexicans did as they were told. The fat man twitched on the floor and groaned: Cal, wary, his nerves on a hair-trigger, stepped sideways. He didn't want his legs grabbed too.

Brutus Calhoun's long gunfighter's fingers allied to the knife soon made short work of the rope. The big man rose, grimacing with pain as he chafed his wrists.

He crossed the room and relieved the Mexicans of their hardware, handed Cal an extra gun. Then, while the younker covered the unarmed men, Brute got to work with the knife again and cut the other two men and the girl free.

They stood up slowly, all grimacing as they suffered the agony of returning circulation. Even Nevada managed to stand upright, steadying himself against a packing-case.

Pecos Charlie stepped forward, sections of rope draped over his arm. 'Now lemme tie these jaspers up,' he said, grinning behind his whiskers. 'I learned some real fancy knots when I was a sailor.' He looked round at the assembled company. 'You didn't know I'd been a sailor did yuh? Yeh, that's where I lost this laig. A shark made a meal of it.'

Nobody knew whether to believe the old buzzard or not, but at least his humour served to break the almost murderous tension. The old marshal made good his boast anyway: by trussing the four Mexicans like turkey-cocks with the meagre lengths of frayed rope he had at his disposal. They were gagged with their own bandannas and laid in a row among the dirty boxes. The four men and the girl sorted their own weapons out and added one apiece from the Mex collection for good measure.

'Now let's get them horses,' growled Nevada and made an experimental parabola on his wounded leg.

They eyed him critically. 'You sure you'll be all right, oldtimer?' asked Brute Calhoun.

'Sure I'm sure. I'd do yuh a little dance if I had time.'

'Let's go then,' said Marshal Heckerstein and led the way.

After receiving instructions from Brutus, they split up into two sections so they would not be too conspicuous if they bumped into any roisterers from the cantina. The sound of revelry was wafted to them: not everybody at the settlement was a member of Joaquin's grim mob.

Brute went with Nevada, the latter leaning on the big man's arm. Biddy, Pecos Charlie and Cal made a detour. Following Brutus's directions the little band planned to come together again at the stables.

Gun in hand, Cal led the way. Biddy was almost at

his elbow. She held her gun as purposefully as any man. Cal had no doubt that, if need be, she would start shooting; and a durnsight more effectively, probably, than he could himself. The thought of violence in connection with this slim figure stirred him strangely. For a moment he had a great sense of unreality, so that it seemed he was standing apart, watching three other people creeping stealthily through the dark night.

Who was this girl? Was he just dreaming and was she just the ghost of another girl. . . ?

. . . Maybe if he had not had this strange detached feeling he would have seen the man sooner. He was a big man and he came quickly round the corner of some kind of outhouse and, before Cal could hide his gun, had spotted it.

He gave a guttural exclamation and went for his own gun. Cal had never thought so fast in his life. The distance between the two of them was so great that he could not slug the man before the shooting began. If he hesitated he would lose the advantage he already had. The man would start shooting . . .

The stranger's gun was half out of its holster when Cal lowered his own gun a fraction and pressed the trigger. The man let his gun fall, clapped both hands to his punctured thigh, did a crazy little dance, then fell flat on his back. All the time, however, he was squealing like a stuck pig, making the night hideous with his cries.

Pecos Charlie stepped swiftly past Cal and his arm rose and fell. There was a dull *clump* and the man became silent. But the damage had already been done. Around at the cantina a suddenly opened door released an alarming gush of sound. Voices shouted, boot heels thudded on hard sod.

'Sorry I had to do that,' said Cal Mackey, and he was moving again.

'There was nothing else you could do,' said the marshal.

'Just rank bad luck,' panted Biddy.

'This way.' Cal was again in the lead.

They reached the door of the stables to find Brutus and Nevada already there. The tall man, a gun in each hand, was half crouched, peering into the night. Nevada was propped against one post of the door and he had a gun in each hand, too.

'I had to shoot somebody,' said Cal. 'Just busted his laig, but he hollered like I'd shot his nose off, till Charlie put him to sleep.'

'Yeh, we heard him hollering,' said Nevada. 'Heck of a lot of echoes now, too.'

Lights bobbed, coming nearer to the stables. Voluble Spanish voices made the night hideous with questions and curses.

Brute, with a muttered word to Nevada, had disappeared into the gloom of the stables. Cal and the marshal followed him. Biddy took up her stand beside the old man. They worked like a team now – all five of them. None of the men now were uncertain about the woman, her attitude to violence and danger. She played her equal part and they took that part for granted. It was the greatest compliment they could ever have paid her.

The three men returned leading the horses.

110

Nevada was helped on to his. The flaming torches came nearer, flamed brighter. Brutus fired a couple of shots over the people's heads and they fell back a little. But, as the little calvalcade thundered from the yard, answering bullets came perilously close.

The shooting swelled. Riding was perilous. It was because of this, the hideous din, the danger, the breakneck riding, that the five riders did not see the other bunch of horsemen until they were almost upon them.

By then it was too late and pretty soon they were surrounded and engulfed by the superior numbers of Joaquin and his men.

CHAPTER XII

Joaquin's voice rang out above the din and angry men backed away from the captives, all of whom realized by now that Verez and his *segunda* had not been found.

The circle widened but there was no break in it. Others on foot ran to swell its ranks and the torchlight gleamed and flickered on angry faces.

The four men and the girl were grouped close together. They were all a little dishevelled but had no new hurts. Old Nevada was still cursing monotonously, but, with gentlemanly delicacy, quite mildly. Somebody had bumped his leg. Cal Mackey's head felt like somebody was hitting it rhythmically with a huge padded mallet. It was a sensation not very conducive to clear thinking. He felt like blasting away at all these dark yammering faces, but, in any case, he had lost his gun and all his pards – Biddy included – had been relieved of their hardware, too.

The shouting and the threats died down as Joaquin kneed his horse into the centre of the circle, brought himself face to face with Brutus Calhoun.

'You could not wait until we returned, could you?' he said. 'You knew we would not find Manuel and Pablo.'

'We were prisoners,' retorted Brutus. 'Prisoners are privileged to escape if a chance occurs.' He added sardonically, 'If you had put us on our honour maybe we would have waited till your return.'

'Honour,' sneered Joaquin. 'What do you know about honour? You were too eager to get back to your gold, to take it away with you, split it among you.'

It was an admirable grandstand blow and awakened an angry murmur from the swelling ranks of the onlookers. Already they were chafing again. And if they did suddenly take a hand in the game things would undoubtedly go ill with the five people trapped in the circle. But Joaquin's presence carried weight and Joaquin had not yet finished his perorations.

'It's all very clear now,' he cried. 'You were after Slack McGee because you wanted the gold. But Manuel and Pablo had already caught up with McGee and taken the gold from him. So you killed Manuel and Pablo . . .'

'And came right back here to tell you all about it!' broke in Brutus jeeringly. 'You don't make sense, *amigo*.' His voice rang out. 'You are playing some deep game of your own. I think maybe you would like to take Manuel's place as boss of this territory.'

This caused a stir in the ranks. But Joaquin quelled it by raising his one arm. There was something about this lean, intense one-armed *caballero* that commanded attention. The presence of Brutus was even more commanding, his big body radiated power, his voice had an organ-like resonance. But, this time, everything was in the other man's favour and in this the gunman-preacher had met his match.

'You cannot cover your own evil by slander and lies,' said Joaquin.

Brutus said: 'You found the body of the outlaw. Where is the body?'

'We found no body.'

'Who is lying now?'

But Joaquin had no need to answer this. Matu, the Indian boy, kneed his horse forward. 'It is true what he says, Señor Calhoun.'

'Then maybe the man was not killed after all. Or McGee took the body away with him. Surely you do not think we murdered Manuel and Pablo, Matu?'

The Indian boy did not answer, but turned his horse away again and even Brutus realized the weakness of his own argument. The sullen murmuring was beginning to rise again as Joaquin also turned his horse away from the circle, joined the ranks of his men before speaking again.

'Are any of you going to tell us where Manuel and Pablo are?'

'None of us know where they are,' spoke up Marshal Heckerstein. 'All Brutus has told you is true.'

Cal Mackey had regained his wits. He shouted hotly above the rising noise. 'I believe something else Brutus has said. You don't really want Manuel and Pablo back, you just want to turn yourself into a big hero and take over.'

Nevada did not actually add anything to the conversation, but was heard by those nearest to him to let forth a string of oaths among which Joaquin's name was interspersed. Biddy did not say anything. She sat erect in the saddle, her chin up, as if she despised these dark-faced creatures who milled around her.

Their hot eyes were fixed upon her and she felt very vulnerable, and not a little scared. But not for the world would she reveal that fact.

Her lips curled. She had not intended to speak, but finally could not stem the words which burst involuntarily from her lips.

'For all your talk of honour and justice you're just a pack of thieves and murderers, and that man,' she pointed dramatically at Joaquin, 'is the biggest rogue of you all. Do you intend to follow him like a flock of mangy sheep?'

Her words rang in the sudden stillness. A few pairs of dark eyes glowed with admiration; there was still a certain amount of old-world Spanish courtesy about these people. They admired a spirited woman. For a moment even Joaquin seemed nonplussed. But one of his cohorts suddenly came to his rescue, riding up beside him, muttering something in his ear.

Joaquin smiled his thin, mirthless smile. In the flickering torchlight he looked almost ghoulish. He kneed his horse a little way forward again.

He jerked his thumb as he shouted, 'Santos here has just told me something that is very interesting. This fine young lady who is giving herself such airs was, before she started riding with Brutus Calhoun and his men, an employee of Frisco Lil's in San Antone. A faro girl, a cheap clip-joint filly!'

Both Cal and Brutus started forward at this insult to their female companion. But they were brought up short by the menacing guns.

'It's true what I say,' put in the worthy Santos. 'Many a time I've seen her.'

'That's right. I thought I'd seen her someplace before!' The speaker this time was an unshaven American, a filthy-looking renegade if ever there was one. His bleary eyes shone, his stump teeth gnashed. He was proud of being the centre of attraction for once.

'I seen her,' he yammered. 'I even played on her table once. She's a smarty, she fleeced me all right . . .'

'That's a lie!' Biddy's voice was shrill with rage. She had her dander up and once more Cal and the boys saw the pugnacious virago they had first met at Frisco Lil's.

'You filthy lying scum!' She kneed her horse forward furiously. Her movement was so unexpected that she was beside her accuser before anybody could stop her. Her spirited pony, snorting, charged the other's flea-bitten nag.

The horse staggered, the saddle-tramp, his unshaven face suddenly alarmed, swayed in the saddle. Biddy's small clenched fist against his face completed the job. The renegade tumbled ignominiously to the dust.

Somebody laughed. But there were cries of rage, too. When the unshaven man rose his gun was in his hand. Joaquin kicked him viciously on the side of the head and he went down again. His gun was lost in the dust; he lay still this time.

Another man pushed his horse forward and grabbed the bridle of the girl's mount. She struck out at him and missed. He raised his own fist, then changed his mind.

Joaquin had his gun levelled at the four horsemen in the centre of the circle.

'You wouldn't like your friends to be shot down like dogs would you, *chiquita*?' he shouted. He leered at her; it was pretty obvious he meant what he said.

Biddy quietened down, drew her horse in line with those of her friends. 'She needs ducking in the river to cool her off,' yelled somebody. By her show of temper she had not done herself or her friends any good. But they did not blame her for that and Pecos Charlie, who was nearest, said, 'Good for you, gel.'

The crowd was jostling and growling again. They had seen violence and it had awakened the beast in them – the beast that lurks in all crowds. They were not individuals any more: they were one pulsing, monstrous heart, stirred by a brave woman fighting tooth and nail like a man – but stirred in the wrong way.

The shifting, flickering light of the torches lit the scene garishly, wickedly. The press became greater around the four people trapped in the middle of the circle like rats in a pit.

Joaquin's good arm rose. He fired his gun in the air and, as the echoes rolled away, there was an uneasy silence once more, a silence that was full of ominous little sounds and movements; the sputter of the torches, the champing of horses, the movements of their feet and of human feet, the chinking of bridles, the sibilant breathing of men under stress of violent emotion . . .

Joaquin's voice rose. 'Once more I am giving these people a chance to answer my question. Any one of them. I will even go so far as to say we will be lenient with the one who talks . . .'

He paused dramatically. Then he moved his horse again, so that he was a little nearer to the prisoners, so that he could be more clearly seen by everybody.

'Two questions,' he shouted. Then he faced the prisoners directly. 'Where are Manuel and Pablo? Where is the gold?'

'Shouldn't you have put the second question first?' retorted Brute Calhoun. 'Your eyes are shining with greed. Wouldn't you be disappointed, too, if we suddenly told we *did* know where Manuel and Pablo are and that they are still alive and kicking? With them dead and the gold in your greedy paws as well you'd have things pretty much the way you wanted them, wouldn't you?'

It was a last desperate bid to sway the crowd's temper in the other direction, or at least to make it more rational. But things had gone too far now. They hardly heard the last part of Brute's words – the fact that he had spoken at all, without answering Joaquin's question, only antagonized them – they bayed for blood once more.

Joaquin waved his arms again but it was some minutes before the clamour died down. He had played his cards well. He had got the mob at fever-pitch. They were in a mood to condone anything he chose to do. Yes, and take a bloody part in it, too.

'A man has been shot,' shouted Joaquin. 'Others of our men have been roughed around by these people in trying frantically to escape. And then they expect us to believe that they had no hand in the disappearance of Manuel and Pablo, of Slack McGee and the Government gold. We have a swift justice here. We also have ways of making people talk. We show no mercy with back-shooting skunks – or their fancy dance-hall women.'

The roar that greeted the end of Joaquin's pretty little speech was not unlike the baying of angry timber-wolves.

'Over to the barn with them!' yelled somebody.

A chorus of assent greeted these words. Evidently the barn had exciting associations for these owlhooters of the settlement. Maybe it contained the local execution block – or something similar.

The whole mob surged forward. Only the presence of Joaquin and the other mounted men prevented the prisoners from being roughly handled.

The barn was reached. The cavalcade halted beneath the upper door of the hay-loft. Here a stout beam of wood stuck outwards, silhouetted against the night sky. There was a pulley at the end of it; no doubt the whole thing was just a single contrivance for hauling up sacks of fodder. But it could be used for another procedure, almost as simple – but far more horrifying.

The tumult died suddenly. The prisoners realized that the beam had, indeed, been used for other purposes.

'The old man first,' said Joaquin. 'We'll put him out of his misery.'

'Why, you filthy skunk!' Cal Mackey kneed his horse forward. Brutus Calhoun was right at his side, his usually inscrutable features almost demoniacal with rage. Hands struck at them. They were forced back at the point of menacing guns.

Nevada and his mount were hustled beneath the beam. A rope was thrown across it. There was a horrified gasp from Biddy. Somebody had already made a hangman's noose.

The noose was placed around Nevada's neck. He cursed his captors levelly, without fear, and with an admirably virulent turn of phrase.

Joaquin had a heavy watch in his hand. 'If somebody doesn't tell us what we want to know in the space of three minutes the old man swings.'

There was a sudden commotion in the ranks behind him. Matu, the Indian youth, rode forward.

'You cannot do this,' he cried. 'The master would not want it this way. You have no proof of guilt, the master always wanted proof.'

Joaquin spoke gruffly to a man beside him, who grabbed the bridle of Matu's horse. The Indian boy struck out with a clenched fist and the man went down. But, in an instant, two more men had closed around the Indian, so that, for a moment, he was hidden from the crowd. There was the sickening sound of a heavy blow, and when the group broke up

120

again Matu's horse was riderless. The Indian boy lay in the dust. They left him there.

Old Nevada sat erect in the saddle with the noose around his neck. A man stood at the horse's rump with a quirt dangling in his hand. No flicker of fear showed on the old man's face in the light of the torches. If his leg pained him, he did not reveal this fact by word or gesture.

'After the slight delay I will start timing again,' said Joaquin, holding his turnip-watch ostentatiously in front of him. 'Is anybody going to talk'? Are you going to talk, old man?'

Nevada spat but did not quite reach his target. 'Go to hell,' he said.

The man with the quirt raised it above the horse's flanks. Joaquin, motionless, held the watch before him. Both Cal and Brutus tried to break free again but they were hemmed in by menacing steel.

'You can't do this,' burst out Marshal Heckerstein. 'I am the law. I say you can't do this.'

It was a dramatic but useless appeal. 'Here *we* are the law,' said Joaquin.

There was silence, a tenseness of dark faces, a concentration of eyes shining in the torchlight. In a split second the quirt would fall and Nevada would be jerked to eternity.

The diversion came not from inside the mob this time, but from outside of it. Hoofs clattered. Voices shouted.

Heads were turned. The mob milled like frightened steers in a thunderstorm. Even Joaquin was startled, non-plussed. He lowered his watch, turned his head. Attention was away from the prisoners for a moment. Brutus, taller even than Cal Mackey, rose in his stirrups and took the rope from around Nevada's neck. The old man said 'Thanks' with a gusty sigh. The Mexican with a quirt started forward, going for his gun. Cal Mackey reached out a long leg and kicked him viciously beneath the chin.

He went down. The horses milled over him. Joaquin had his back to the prisoners now. Somebody shouted, 'It's Manuel!'

CHAPTER XIII

The ranks parted and Verez and Pablo, both very dishevelled-looking, rode through. Matu was being helped to his feet by two men. His face was dirty, hideously bloodstained. His eyes stared as he thrust the men away from him and staggered towards his 'master'.

Manuel had eyes only for the Indian boy.

'What is this? What does this mean?' It was the old thundering voice of the scourge of the Rio Grande. It was years since folks had seen Verez in such a murderous rage. Behind him, Pablo, his face inscrutable, sat with his hand on the butt of his gun. It was evident that, if anybody got rough, Pablo was good and ready to start shooting.

Matu caught hold of Manuel's stirrup. His mouth twisted and moved as he tried to find words, but he was still only half-conscious. Verez turned angrily on Joaquin.

'What has happened?'

Joaquin was still non-plussed. He could only look

about him as if there were a good many questions he, too, wished to ask. But there was nobody there who would answer them for him.

Brutus Calhoun kneed his horse forward. 'I will tell you what has happened, Manuel.'

Verez seemed to see the prisoners for the first time. His sharp eyes raked their faces, showing no astonishment at the sight of the girl, before returning once more to Brutus.

'*Amigo.*' He held out his hand and Brutus took it.

Then Manuel turned away suddenly, stood upright in his stirrups and raised his hands.

'I want everybody armed and at their usual places. I want guards at the river. I have a sneaking idea that The Wolf may pay us a visit tonight.'

At this a babble of talk broke out. Verez turned to Pablo. 'See that everybody does as they should.'

'Right, Manuel.' The *segunda* forced his horse through the press, began to bawl orders.

Verez summoned two more men to look after Matu. 'We will all go to the hacienda,' he said.

Although Pablo had always delighted in joshing the Indian boy, Matu was his friend, too. So, as soon as Manuel Verez had disappeared into the dark with the prisoners, his *segunda* turned on Joaquin and began to shoot questions at him.

The one-armed man had regained his customary sang froid. He talked fast.

He had a very glib tongue. He had discovered also, long ago, that because he only had one arm people forgave him his cantankerous temper. In

124

fact, he was not at all cantankerous, but coldly calculating. His temper was a pose. It made lesser men fear him and others shake their heads pityingly, condoning his irascibility, labelling him a 'character', as Verez was a character, and Pablo, and The Wolf.

He told Pablo that he had given him and Verez up for dead, foully murdered by Brutus Calhoun and his gang. He was sorry Matu had been hurt, but the boy was so obstreperous, Joaquin had thought him blinded by his old boyish hero-worship of the tall gunman. Joaquin was still of the opinion there was something fishy about Brutus. Why had the big man tried to make everyone believe that he had reformed, turned preacher? Was it not possible that, under this guise, he was working hand-in-glove with the pestilent Slack McGee?

Pablo, who had been quite prepared to shoot the one-armed man in the guts, now found himself being tangled up in Joaquin's glib rhetoric. Other folks were asking questions, too, even while they obeyed the orders they had been given.

Why had the settlement to be turned suddenly into an armed camp?

The story Pablo had to tell was not complimentary to Manuel and himself; but he did not shirk it.

Slack Mc Gee and his two pardners had given them the slip, had doubled back on their tracks, no mean feat when one took into consideration old Manuel's reputation as a tracker. No doubt it was true then that the three men had laid an ambush for Brute Calhoun and his party. Manuel and Pablo had been picking up the trail again when they had run into another bunch of horsemen, a sizable one which, if Pablo did not miss his guess, belonged to The Wolf. Anyway, the two old friends, with slugs buzzing around them, had to beat a hasty retreat.

They had outstripped their pursuers but had almost run into more riders. They had not seen them, had only heard them. Maybe it had been the Slack McGee party. If so the latter were calculated to ride smack into The Wolf party: a bad thing for both McGee and the Government gold.

Manuel had been of the opinion that the larger party was on its way to another attack on the riverside settlement. Their meeting with Slack McGee might hold them up a little, but not for long, hence the warlike preparations. . . .

The rest of the men were satisfied, and went about their business. But Joaquin still lingered. He was a mean and stubborn cuss, he still seemed to think he had done right in planning to string up Brute Calhoun and his companions.

Pablo's eyes narrowed. 'Would you have hanged the woman, Joaquin?' he asked.

'I think one of them would've talked before we got to that stage,' said Joaquin. He preened himself. 'I think I knew what I was doing, Pablo.'

Pablo decided that he did not like Joaquin. That, in fact, he had never liked Joaquin. Maybe there was something in what Brute Calhoun had said, something about Joaquin wanting to be top-dog, to take the place of Manuel, of Pablo.

Joaquin always had had a chip on his shoulder. He had the reputation of a gunman, too, could shoot far better with one hand than many men could with two.

The volatile Pablo looked Joaquin up and down. Maybe the one-armed man was a snake-in-the-grass. He had the appearance of one anyway.

Joaquin, in his turn, watched Pablo, and still made no attempt to move. Maybe he still wanted to vindicate himself, for Pablo to tell him he had been right in what he had planned to do. Then again, maybe he had some inkling of what was going on in Pablo's mind. These two men, who had ridden together many times, faced each other now like two strange dogs. A growl from one of them might precipitate a fight.

They were two very dissimilar men. Pablo liked things straight-forward. He was ruthless but had no cunning and treachery in his make-up. He loved fighting for the sheer love of fighting. If a man wanted to fight – even if that man had once been a friend – well, Pablo would fight him; and no questions asked. Joaquin had a gun there, stripped low to his waist, within good reach of his good arm. If Joaquin suddenly felt enmity toward Pablo, or an enmity that lay hidden and smouldering had now flared up, all he had to do was go for that gun, and Pablo would endeavour to accommodate him as a fighting man should; and no pinking him in the arm or shoulder like a fancy dan either. Pablo knew Joaquin was fast, mighty fast. But he'd take his chances: a man had to die sometime and to die in action was the best way as far as Pablo was concerned.

CHAPTER XIV

Joaquin, he was different, his was the tortuous mind of a serpent. He did covet Pablo's job, had done so for a long time. The right-hand man of Manuel Verez had a great inheritance if only he played his cards right: it grieved and angered Joaquin that Pablo, the cloddish oaf, did not seem aware of this fact. Joaquin was not a direct man. He had only been ruthlessly direct as leader of a lynching party because it had suited him to do so. But he preferred stealth and circumspection.

In a way, Pablo had him in a corner now, and Joaquin's pride would not let him back down. He realized that if he wanted to take Pablo's place this was his chance; he might never have another one like it. The men had rallied to his call. Brutus Calhoun would be swinging from a beam now if Manuel and Pablo had not returned. Joaquin had been surprised at their return. It was Manuel's presence that had changed things, not Pablo's. The old wolf had lost none of his power. But if he, Joaquin, killed Pablo in fair fight, could Manuel victimise him for it, would not he be the only one to take Pablo's place? Even if, in Manuel's eyes, he had made a mistake tonight had he not proved that he could handle the men as well as Pablo? Nay, better than Pablo, who often was just a drunken fool, too familiar with the men: far more familiar than Joaquin, though he was only a storekeeper, had ever been.

But Pablo was now cold-sober, and when sober he was greased-lightning with a gun. Joaquin did not know whether he could beat Pablo.

Joaquin was not afraid of pain or of death. Maybe, most of all, he was afraid of failure, of the cup of power which he had so recently sipped being taken from his lips forever. He was not a gambler. He preferred to wait until the cards were stacked in his favour.

But would Pablo allow him to wait?

The thoughts sped through his mind and Pablo was watching him all the time. Was Pablo waiting for him to go, to obey orders the way the others had done? Or was it too late to go now, was the invisible gauntlet already thrown down there between them, could Joaquin turn away now without having to appear that he had backed down? Joaquin knew that although the erstwhile lynch-mob had ostensibly split up, hastened to fortify the settlement, many of them were still hanging around in the shadows. Many of them had felt the weight of Pablo's hands, the lash of his virulent and forthright tongue. They did not expect Joaquin, who only a few moments ago had held them all in the palm of his single hand, had swayed them with his presence, to back down meekly before Pablo.

Pablo was pressing him now, the very look of Pablo, the very presence of him. The tension was in the air all around them.

And finally Pablo spoke, silkily.

'Why do you stand there, Joaquin? Have you more to say?'

'I think you and Manuel trust Brute Calhoun too much.'

'And because you do not trust him you wish to hang him, huh? That is harsh treatment, *amigo*.'

Joaquin gave a characteristic shrug. 'Not to hang these people now maybe. But to keep them prisoner, make them talk.'

Pablo's eyes glowed with evil mirth. 'So now you have changed your mind, Joaquin. You are being lenient.'

'When I planned to hang them it was because I thought they had killed you and Manuel.' Joaquin lifted a hand. He saw Pablo stiffen. He let the hand fall with a little slap to his side. Pablo was slouching, it was almost as if he was falling slowly into a crouch. Joaquin went on:

'Now I know you and Manuel are well . . .' He left the sentence unfinished. He shrugged again, but this time did not raise his hand.

'Do not tell me you would grieve for Manuel and myself,' Pablo leered. He was openly taunting Joaquin now and the watching shadows were coming nearer.

Nobody could ever have called Joaquin a coward.

The time for circumspection was past. He said:

'I would not grieve for you, Pablo. I should not care if you were buzzard meat right now.'

'Maybe you would like to try and make me that way,' said Pablo.

He crouched lower now and his gun-hand was a claw. His eyes shone exultantly in the half-light.

The feet scraped softly and the shadows became men and then there was silence.

'A man can take but so much,' said Joaquin, and he went for his gun.

You watch a man's eyes, not his gun-hand. Joaquin saw Pablo's eyes widen. They blazed with fierce exultation, they filled the whole world, they made the night flame with their exultant triumph. Joaquin had seen Pablo's eyes flame like that before, he had seen Pablo kill men before. Pablo's eyes were the eyes of a killer, a *caballero* who gave a man an even break; but killed for the love of killing for all that.

Even as his fingers closed over his gun, Joaquin knew that he had gambled and lost. He hardly felt the bullets hit him. The scalding pain came afterwards but it was all over very quickly.

Manual Verez had finished the story told to Brutus Calhoun and his companions when they heard the two shots. When they reached the scene of the battle Joaquin's body was already being taken away to await burial. His gun was still hooked incongruously on the rim of its holster where his stiffening fingers had left it.

'He was a pig,' said Pablo and spat. 'He wanted you and I dead, *el patrio*. He wanted Brutus and his

132

friends dead. No doubt he wanted Slack McGee dead, too, and the Government gold all to himself. He wanted too much.' Pablo chuckled. 'No doubt he would want The Wolf dead, too.' He flung out his arms. 'Everybody dead. Everybody but Joaquin. . . .'

He paused. Manuel was eyeing him angrily. He added, as if as an afterthought, 'He went for his gun first.' He looked around him. 'Is not that true, my friends?'

Yes, it was true, they said. Who would not back this dangerous man up, true or not?

'How is Matu, Manuel?' asked Pablo innocently.

Verez knew that Pablo was indirectly reminding him of what Joaquin had done to the Indian boy. He smiled thinly. The wicked fox.

'Matu is much better, Pablo.' He rounded then on the men. 'Back to your posts all of you . . . Pablo, is the picket along the river?'

'If it is not it should be. I will find out.' Pablo spun on his heels and hurried into the darkness, the perfect second-in-command.

'Shall we follow him down to the river?' suggested Brutus Calhoun.

'We may as well,' said Verez, and led the way.

Then he halted, turning towards Biddy. 'Maybe it is best that the *señorita* should not come. Lead may fly.'

'Where the boys go I go,' said Biddy sweetly. 'Besides, I'm no stranger to flying lead.'

'That's a fact,' said Nevada admiringly. The oldtimer was limping along without help now.

'Maybe you would like to go back and look after

Matu, Miss Biddy,' suggested Marshal Heckerstein.

'Matu's not badly hurt. He's quite capable of looking after himself.'

'Then you won't go back and look after Matu?'

'No, I won't.'

Pecos Charlie grinned. 'I didn't think you would.'

No more was said.

The Rio looked oily and turgid in the light of the pale moon peeping from behind the clouds. From the cover of rock outcrops along the banks heads bobbed, voices greeted Verez.

'We planted those outcrops ourselves,' said the chief. 'Carrying the stuff from other parts of the territory. They make excellent breastworks.'

'They certainly do,' said Pecos Charlie. 'Anyway, I would've figured they'd been there since creation.'

Verez went on: 'This stretch of the river is the shallowest part. We keep it well-guarded. The Wolf's men may try to cross. If they do they'll get a hot reception. The Wolf's had that experience once before though – as you can see, there's not much cover the other side of the river. I don't think the skunk will try it again. He'll probably swim his horses and men across the river higher up, where it's deeper. I've got pickets here and there, but naturally we can't patrol all the river. Still, there's open land all around the settlement – it was cleared purposely except for the river approach here. Even if The Wolf gets over the river he's not likely to be able to creep up on us unseen.'

'You old fox,' said Brutus with a grim smile. 'And I'd back the fox against the wolf this time.'

Verez bowed slightly. 'Thank you, *amigo*.' But his voice was grave. 'You've never met The Wolf?'

'No, only heard about him.'

'He is not a man to be taken lightly.'

'Have you met him?'

Verez smiled thinly. 'Not exactly face to face. I still look forward to that happy day.'

He looked about him. 'Everything is well-organized here. We will walk around the settlement.'

They retraced their steps. Manuel and Brutus, Pecos Charlie and Nevada, Cal and Biddy. Cal wondered if the girl, walking so straight, so quietly at his elbow, felt any strangeness at her surroundings. The stillness of the waiting men, the gurgle of the river, the atmosphere of violence and sudden death. She was probably the only woman at the moment in the settlement, except for a few aged squaws. He felt that, in some way, he should be protecting her. But she did not need his protection.

How would Lucinda have comported herself in such a situation? The thought of her still gave him pain, but it was duller now. And he found he could not answer the question he had put himself.

The lights were dim. There was little to be heard but the soughing of the wind, until they got nearer to the shacks.

Footsteps sounded, came nearer to them. A lithe figure, limping a little, came out of the dusk. It was Matu, his eyes shining from between folds of bandages.

'You shouldn't be out of bed,' said Verez.

'I feel all right now, master. I wish to be of help.'

'There isn't much you can do now, son. All we can do is wait.'

Matu's white teeth flashed. 'I can shoot.' He paused, then added reflectively, 'I heard shooting.'

'Pablo and Joaquin had a gunfight. Joaquin was killed.'

'And Pablo?'

Verez shrugged. 'What do you think, little one?'

'Joaquin was evil,' said Matu. He fell into step with the rest of the bunch.

A sound had been impinging itself upon the consciousness of all of them over the last few minutes, and, as Matu's voice died, the sound became more insistent. It was a high keening, like the sound of an animal in pain.

'For Pete's sake,' said Nevada. 'What is that? I've heard a good many different species of coyote – but that beats me.'

Even Verez looked puzzled. Then Matu said, 'I think it is Joaquin's Indian boy, Little Beaver, mourning over his dead master. He is but an ignorant savage.'

Beside him Cal Mackey felt the girl shudder. He said, 'Can't you make him shut up?'

'I will try,' said Matu and hurried forward.

The rest of them followed more slowly. Verez said, 'Yes, now I remember Joaquin's Indian boy. He served in the cantina.'

'I think we all saw him when we came here first,' said Brute Calhoun.

'He worshipped Joaquin,' said Verez.

'As Matu worships you.'

'Matu is my son,' said Verez, a little stiffly. 'He is very intelligent, well-educated. There is a great bond between us. This boy is, as Matu said, still an ignorant savage.'

'There was a bond between Joaquin and him, too, though.'

Verez nodded his head gravely. 'It is a pity.'

The keening had stopped, but now, as they got nearer to the shacks they could hear hurried voices. One of the voices belonged to Matu. The other was shriller, younger, it sobbed, expostulated, rose to anger. There were running footsteps, the clatter of a horse's hoofs.

Verez darted forward. Despite his age, he was very spry. The other men, although they followed his example, were still behind him as he rounded the corner of the shack. A horseman sped away into the dark, vanished from sight, hoofbeats fading away in the stillness. Light streamed through the open door-way of the shack. Verez passed through it and the others followed. Biddy had caught them up now, was joggling Cal's arm.

They entered the lighted shack, spread themselves out behind Verez. It was a strange sight that met their eyes.

Matu, his bandage awry, his face bleeding, was clambering to his feet. 'He got away,' gasped the Indian boy. 'He got away.' He staggered towards them. 'We must stop him.'

None of the others moved. They seemed rooted to the spot.

The little shack was bare, except for a few old

boxes and miscellaneous items of junk. It had evidently been used at some time for some kind of storeroom but had been let to go to ruin, and by the look of things was now used as a sort of unofficial undertaking parlour. There were black curtains up at the single window. A fitful light came from a small hurricane-lantern dangling from the ceiling, making the shadows in the corners writhe like unidentifiable beasts waiting to pounce. In the centre of the room were three trestles. Two of them were upright and empty, looked as if they had been scrubbed clean quite recently. The other one was also empty, but had been overturned.

Its late occupant lay on the floor beside it, quite close to the spot from which Matu had picked himself up. He had, no doubt, brought the trestle over with him when falling. And there was Joaquin, flat on his back, his sightless eyes staring up at the ceiling, a horrible disappointed leer on his face. He had known what was happening to him, all of it at the end, had Joaquin. And the knowledge had been bitter as gall.

Cal Mackey felt Biddy's fingers tighten involuntarily on his arm. No, Joaquin was not a pretty sight. His breast was dyed red. It did not look like blood anymore, but paint. He looked like a man-size broken doll thrown carelessly there, splashed with paint. And, strangely enough, his very lifelessness seemed the most horrible thing of all.

Verez took two quick strides forward, put his foot to the body and rolled it over on its face. Then he turned towards Matu who now stood uncertainly between Nevada and Pecos Charlie, dabbing his bleeding face with a red and white 'kerchief the latter had given him.

'What happened?'

'When I came in Little Beaver was on his knees, bent over the body. His hands were covered with blood. He was wailing, but he heard me come in and stopped and turned his head. I told him to shut up and come away, that the master had ordered he come away. He cursed me in his own dialect. He said my master's man had killed his master, his blood-brother, and that he hated my master and all of us. He said that the blood of Joaquin cried out for vengeance and he would be the instrument of vengeance . . .'

'Crazy kid,' said Cal Mackey.

'But he would really believe that,' said Verez gravely.

'Little Beaver *did* believe it,' intoned Matu. 'I tried to reason with him, but he would not listen. He turned back to his master, dappled his hands on his master's blood and painted it on his own chest. He was beginning to cry again. I took him by the shoulders, gently, but he turned on me and in his hand was a knife. We grappled for the knife and I hit my head on the edge of the trestle and turned it over. I was dazed. I felt as if suddenly I was fighting Joaquin, too. Before I could regain my senses he had got away. I am sorry, master. I . . .'

'Do not blame yourself, son,' put in Verez gently. 'You were in no condition for fighting. Anyway, what can Little Beaver do?'

'Maybe he hopes to join up with The Wolf, to help The Wolf to get to us.'

Verez smiled thinly. 'He can try. But he has to get out of the settlement first, across the river. Maybe one of the guards will stop him.'

'I am all right now. I will ride after him.' Matu started for the door.

Verez grabbed his arm. 'You will stay here. We will look for Little Beaver.'

Biddy took over. She grabbed Matu's arm. 'You can come back with me to the hacienda, my bully-boy. That bandage wants fixing.'

Matu allowed himself to be led away. Between them the men got the trestle upright and Joaquin's body back upon it. This time they covered the body with an old blanket. Verez, the last to leave, blew out the lamp and closed the door behind him.

They went and got their horses and rode along the river. None of the pickets had seen the runaway Indian boy. 'We must make a detour and get across higher up,' said Verez, and they rode back to the settlement.

They then went to the hacienda and partook of a supper jointly prepared by Matu and Biddy.

'The gel kin cook, too,' said old Nevada admiringly as he champed on succulent pot-roast. He winked at Cal and the younker felt himself flushing. He realized that at times he lost sight of the main object of their long ride and he hated himself for it. Again he reminded himself, punished himself, studiously ignored this other girl.

But she was so fresh and wholesome and lovely,

friendly without being coquettish. He was a healthy young plainsman. He found it hard to ignore her. The dead are dead and it is hard to ignore the living.

Afterwards the five men went out once more on patrol. Matu and Biddy, despite protests, promised to join them as soon as they had done the washing-up.

The night wore on and there was a tenseness about the camp. Men stiffened and raised their guns when a coyote howled, a horse whinnied or moved restlessly. The moon was no help. It kept drifting behind black clouds. Men found their vision suddenly obscured as if a dark blanket had suddenly fallen on the land. They strained their eyes, peering into a woolliness that frustrated and unnerved them. The wind dropped. The heat become oppressive.

'There is a storm due,' said Verez.

A menacing rumble echoed his words. Men started to their feet, taking the sound for approaching hoofbeats, then subsiding sheepishly as they realized it was only thunder.

But they started again nervously as the heavens were split by a vicious jagged tongue of light and the thunder rumbled again like the jeering laughter of a hidden giant.

The first heavy drops of rain fell, plummetting from the sky to fall in the dust, break into tiny crystals and be swallowed up. Until more came, until there was a solid sheet of rain and the dry ground sucked it up thirstily, and it chuckled as it spread. Men were soaked to the skin in the matter of seconds. A few of them, who had been careful draped themselves in slickers. But none of them left their posts.

Manuel Verez and his party all had slickers tied to their mounts. They made haste to don them. They shouted at each other, but the thunder of the storm drowned their voices. The rain was a blinding sheet now, cutting off vision, too. It made tiny pools in the brims of men's hats, the pools overflowed, causing miniature waterspouts which cascaded over men's faces and down their backs. Weapons were hastily covered up. Many men along the river banks lay belly-down on their rifles to keep them dry.

The rain was savage, brutally elemental, a solid pounding violence. It beat viciously at man and beast, lashed, pounded, stung. Those of the guard who were mounted had to hold on to their frightened horses, pressing lips to silky ears, making soothing noises. The storm had been so sudden, almost like a calculated attack. Nature allying herself with the forces of evil.

Cal Mackey tried to peer through a green lashing curtain. Thousands of tiny knives slashed at his face, so that he cringed from them but could not escape. A horseman hove up beside him and instinctively he was wary. But it was Brute Calhoun, leaning over in the saddle, shouting at the top of his resonant voice.

'I don't expect Biddy and the boy will try to make it in this weather.'

'I guess they're safer in the hacienda, at that,' bawled Cal, as like some kind of elemental spirit a part of the storm, Brutus drifted away from him again.

The thunder crashed, the black clouds were torn apart again and again by jagged gashes of flame, so that ignorant peons cried out in superstition, half expecting the skies to gush blood.

CHAPTER XV

The hoofbeats of racing horses were muffled by the cacaphony of the storm. Gunfire mingled with thunder in a savage cannonade.

'*The Wolf!*' screamed a man.

He choked in his own blood, pitched forward on his face. A friend at his side was seized suddenly by superstitious dread. These riders who had appeared so suddenly were like bats out of hell, spotlighted now and then by the lightning. They were like part of the storm. The man rose, turned to run. A bullet smashed into his spine, jerking him upright in agony, clawing for the skies, momentarily paralyzing him. He was limmed for a moment in the lightning's glow, a tortured effigy, before he crumpled into nothingness.

Gunflashes vied with the lightning. Lead sang upon the hiss of the rain. Gun-thunder put the other kind to shame. The storm was abating a little, but a human storm, attacking now, was far more terrible.

Horses charged hither and thither, some of them

riderless. Men rose to their feet or fired from kneeling positions. Cal Mackey, looking around for his friends, found himself alone. But enemies seemed to be bearing down on him from all sides. He could see them more clearly now: it was as if, now the elements had accomplished their purpose in allowing the attackers to get an advantage, they were drawing away to watch progress.

A horseman rode down upon Cal Mackey. He saw a contorted face, a raised gun. He realized absently that his own gun was in his hand, though he could not remember having drawn it. He fired from the waist and the contorted face disappeared; the man clung for a moment to his horse's neck before tumbling to the sodden ground.

A slug took Cal's hat off. His hair clung wetly to his skull. Turning his head, instinctively, he saw Manuel Verez at his side. The Mexican chief smiled thinly, raised his hand in half salute. The skies were lightening. Cal now spotted others of his friends. Pecos Charlie, Nevada, Brutus.

Something plucked at Cal's shoulder and he turned again. A falling body almost knocked him from the saddle. This time Verez raised his gun in half salute. The attackers were drawing off a little but they had taken their toll before doing so. The bodies of men and horses lay along the river bank.

A man rode to the side of Verez, gesticulating and shouting. Cal Mackey saw the chief's eyes widen. Then he rose in the saddle, twisting his head around as he signalled to Cal, to the marshal, to Nevada. They joined him.

He shouted, 'The Wolf's men split into two sections. The other bunch must've made a detour. They're attacking the settlement, the hacienda . . .'

'Let's go!' said Cal Mackey, and drove spurs into his mount.

As they rode into the dirt stretch which formed the main street of the settlement they were almost attacked by their own men. Had not Verez raised himself in the stirrups and yelled they might have been mown down by Pablo and some of the others. The lean *segunda* joined them.

'This way,' he yelled. 'For a moment I thought we were being attacked from three directions. The other bunch is up by the hacienda and bunkhouse and, if I don't miss my guess, The Wolf's with them.'

'The girl . . .' began Cal Mackey.

'Don't worry,' put in Pablo. 'I already had some men by the hacienda. They'll hold the skunks off till we get there. The Wolf's got some reinforcements from some place. He also took us by surprise. But I think we're beginning to get things in hand now. This time we'll run the skunk straight back to his hole and smoke him out.'

'Pablo, the eternal optimist,' said Verez.

'Optimist, hell!' The *segunda* grinned.

The rain had abated now but still beat sluggishly at the sodden riders in a last sullen attack. The skies were lighter. The men could see each other, hear each other talk plainly. The settlement was ablaze with light now, had the aspect of a garish and rather terrible carnival.

The five men rode full-tilt around the corner of

146

the bunkhouse on to the forecourt of the hacienda. The latter blazed with light, and riding upon it from the other direction was a pack of riders, at their head a batlike figure on a huge black horse.

There was no sound from the hacienda until the front ranks of the attackers got into the light, then the very windows seemed to spit flame. Horses squealed, men were tossed from their backs. The black-clad rider seemed to bear a charmed life. He wheeled his horse, one arm raised as he rallied his men.

Men ran from the bunkhouse and joined Verez and his party. They sent withering fire into the flanks of the attackers, who broke and scattered, taking cover in the shadows. Their leader, still erect in the saddle, brought up the rear, turning his back disdainfully on the defenders.

Covered by their friends, who kept up a withering fire from the bunkhouse, Verez managed to reach the side of the hacienda. A man stepped from the shadows, throwing up his gun, then lowering it again and saluting his chief. The little party dismounted and entered through a side door. They passed through into a front room where Biddy and Matu turned away from a window to greet them. They both had rifles and held them purposefully, so at first glance beneath the light they might have been taken for two determined youths instead of a youth and a girl.

'How many men are there here?' asked Verez quickly.

'There are about a dozen all around the house,' answered Matu.

'Good.' The chief turned to his followers. 'Brutus and Cal, will you stay here? ... Pablo, Nevada, Charlie, come with me.'

The men did as they were told. This was Verez's stronghold and he was chief. It was the way it should be. They respected his judgment, accepted his leadership.

Carrying his rifle, Cal took up his stand beside Biddy at one of the two front windows. Matu and Brutus took the other one.

There was hardly any glass in either of the windows; it was strewn in tiny particles all over the floor. Biddy smiled at Cal, grimly, but without a trace of fear.

He grinned at her. He did not find it hard to grin now. The fire of battle coursed through his veins: he was exultant.

'Howdy,' he said.

'Howdy,' she replied.

Neither of them seemed to be able to add anything more to that. They did not have much more chance anyway. Then:

'Here they come again!' yelled Cal Mackey.

But his sentence was half-lost in a hideous blatter of shooting.

He cradled his rifle to his cheek and started firing. But already the attackers had adopted new tactics. They broke right and left and started to ride Indian-fashion round and round the hacienda at breakneck speed.

The batlike figure of The Wolf on the big black horse halted momentarily before the house as the man urged his minions onwards. Cal Mackey drew a bead, fired, bit off a curse as the bandit-leader's wide-brimmed hat flew off.

The leonine head was limmed for a moment in the light, the unkempt black hair streaming over the ears. The face was as dark as an Indian's and as demoniacal as any painted brave's on the warpath. The Wolf rode down on the house, rode as if he meant to charge straight through the window. But, even as Cal Mackey took another snapshot at him as he wheeled away, disappeared with his men around the corner.

'What a horrible-looking brute,' said Biddy shakily.

'Yeh,' said Cal. He had to admit to himself that he had been a little shaken by the sudden close-up appearance of The Wolf. His nickname certainly fitted him, he looked half-beast.

The attackers were going round and round like savages, and yelling like savages, too, some of them lying flat against the horses' sides so that they were very difficult targets. Cal tried to pick off racing figures and wished he was a better shot. Beside him Biddy was firing steadily. All around him was the din of gunfire, rising to a peak of hideous crescendo.

The lull was so sudden that a man's head was left singing. Then there was a strange scream and the four occupants of that front room turned towards the door, the passage.

Cal Mackey was nearest. He started forward. The door crashed open. A guard staggered in, twisted, fell flat on his back, his sightless eyes staring up at the ceiling. Cal had dropped his rifle; he drew his gun as he stepped over the body. Something that made animal-like sounds came through the doorway like a projectile. Cal was sent spinning. His heel caught against the corpse behind him. A knife missed his throat by a hairs-breadth.

A gun boomed in his ear. From a half-crouching position he saw his attacker wilt, then crumple to a twitching heap which quickly became still.

Matu, a smoking gun in his fist, turned the body over with his foot.

'Little Beaver,' he said softly. 'He must've been the one who helped The Wolf over the river, told him the position of the pickets. Maybe he got his revenge on some of us after all.'

'Looks like he went plumb crazy at the finish,' said Brute Calhoun.

Cal Mackey had moved into the passage, stooped his way through a blue haze of gunsmoke. As he reached the swinging door a man leapt from a horse, ran, half-crouching. He stopped dead as he saw Cal, raised his gunhand. His momentary hesitation cost him his life. Cal fired from the hip. The man pitched forward on his face. A slug took Cal's hat off, another plucked at his sleeve. He took cover once more in the passage, where another of the Verez men joined him.

The firing began to slacken off again, the thundering of hoofs to lessen. Somebody shouted. Suddenly Pablo came running along the passage, another man at his elbow.

'We've driven the river bunch back into the Rio,'

he yelled. 'Our men are cutting at The Wolf from the rear. Let us get after them.'

His voice rang through the suddenly silent hacienda. Then, as if to echo his words, shooting broke out again from outside. But no slugs slammed through windows and into walls.

Verez, Nevada, Charlie, Biddy, Matu and Brutus came away from their posts. 'To the horses,' said the chief, and led the way.

The rain had ceased and now a watery moon came from behind the clouds and bathed the scene in an eerie light. Then, as if everything had been stage-managed to lend a last dramatic intensity to the scene, tongues of flame shot from the bunkhouse. Men spilled out pell-mell.

Pablo caught up with Verez and the rest. The *segunda* was grinning from ear to ear. 'Somebody knocked over a lamp,' he said. 'Still, it's time we had a new bunkhouse. That one was full of bugs.'

'It may spread to the hacienda,' said Verez.

'No. See, *el patrio*, the wind is carrying the flames in the other direction. I have put half a dozen old men fighting the fire. Everybody else wants to go bandit-chasing.'

Indeed, the tables were turned with a vengeance. In the light of the pale moon, with the ruddier glow of the fire, bandits were fleeing towards the river.

And now the erstwhile defenders were in full cry after them, strung out in two long lines, Verez and his newfound friends in the forefront.

Many of The Wolf's men who had been driven

back by the river guards were already wading across the Rio, horses and men harried by snipers' bullets.

The bareheaded batlike figure of the leader on his black horse halted for a moment on the river bank. The Wolf seemed to be making one last attempt to rally his followers. Finally, however, he gave up and urged his horse into the sluggish waters with the rest of them.

They chased The Wolf and his followers into the barren lands beyond the Rio Grande del Norte and on to the foothills. Many of the followers fell by the wayside – the retreat had become a rout – and the others made the foothills and disappeared into the pass.

Here a running battle took place. But The Wolf's men were outnumbered now and were soon in retreat again. The Wolf himself, though he definitely had not fallen by the wayside, seemed to have momentarily vanished.

Verez, riding between Cal Mackey and Pablo, said, 'This trail used to lead to the old San Pueblo Mine until the big land-slide about ten years ago. Unless my memory fails me there is a bottleneck up ahead.'

'You are right, *amigo*,' said Pablo. 'Surely The Wolf does not know of this.'

They turned the bend in the trail and were met by a fusillade of shots. Bullets ricocheted from the rocks and whined away into the darkness.

The firing ceased as soon as it had begun, as the

pursuers hugged the rock wall and quietened terrified horses. As the moon peeped from behind the clouds once more the riders found themselves in a tiny canyon. The walls were smooth and sloping, giving a basin-like effect.

'This was where the landslide occurred,' said Verez.

He sounded surprised, a little awed – as well he might be, for there was not a bandit in sight; the whole bunch seemed to have vanished from the face of the earth.

The party had split into two sections and suddenly somebody shouted. It was Brutus Calhoun's voice. The others found him, joined him. He had Biddy by his side. By now the men were so used to seeing the girl in the thick of the battle that nobody commented on her presence.

'Look,' said Brutus, and pointed upwards.

There was a cleft in the smooth walls of the basin. Disturbed shale betokened the passage of horses.

A rifle cracked suddenly and Brutus's hat fell from his head. One of Verez's men retaliated. Evidently The Wolf had left a guard.

'Come on,' said Cal Mackey, and sent his horse charging at breakneck speed up the slope.

The volatile Pablo was right behind him. The rest of the bunch streamed behind.

There was no more sniping. Evidently the guard had turned and fled. The riders had to descend another, less perilous slope into another even smaller basin which looked like a section of a ghost-town. Shards of broken wood were silhouetted against the pale night sky. Black holes gaped in the ground. The attackers had to slow their horses, the beasts picking their way cautiously over the broken ground. This, then, was the graveyard of the San Pueblo Mine.

Huts were crammed against the far wall of the little basin and it was from there that the firing started again. The attackers dismounted, flinging themselves into cover. Cal and Pablo crouched side by side. The latter said:

'Why did The Wolf lead them into this bottle-neck?'

'Maybe because it gives him a better chance to get away unseen while his followers keep us busy,' said Cal Mackey. 'I haven't spotted the big black skunk lately.'

'No. Nor have I.'

'By now he's probably got Slack McGee's Government gold. That'd be worth running away with.'

There was a lull in the shooting. Pablo began to crawl. Not to be outdone, Cal caught up with him. Behind them the others were doing the same.

Pablo suddenly raised his gun and fired. He cursed. 'I could've sworn I saw a man running over there. He seems to have vanished.'

He changed direction a little, began to crawl in the direction in which he had pointed. Although all Cal Mackey could see was only black rock face – the moonlight did not shine on that end of the basin – his curiosity made him follow Pablo. Anyway, they were moving out of the range of the firing. The bandits were concentrating on the main bulk of the attacking party: there was a chance that Pablo and Cal might be able to creep upon them unobserved.

But, as Pablo and Cal crept nearer to the rock face they made a discovery. The ground dipped suddenly and at the foot of the rock face they saw a hole like the entrance to a cave. This, until they got nearer, had been out of their line of vision.

Shards of broken wood partially blocked the hole, but there was ample room for a man to crawl through. Pablo, who moved like a collection of well-oiled springs, beat Cal to it – which, as things transpired, was lucky for the young rancher.

There was a clatter of loose pebbles and shale. As Cal crawled through a hole in the wake of the Rio hellion a shower of dirt trickled down his neck. Suddenly a gun boomed twice up ahead. The narrow tunnel was lit momentarily with lurid flashes; Pablo cried out with surprise and pain. 'Where'd he get you?' asked Cal.

'In my knee,' grunted Pablo. 'I'm afraid I won't be able to run any more. You get after the skunk. I'll stay here in case he gets past you.'

'Right,' said Cal, and wormed his way past the other man.

He discovered he could stand upright in the tunnel. Keeping his shoulder pressed to one wall, gun in hand, he moved onwards. There was no sound now except the monotonous drip-drip of water from some hidden source. Cal found himself walking on tiptoes. He stopped from time to time to listen. Always he heard tiny sounds. But they could have been made by rats.

The passage seemed to twist and turn endlessly. Maybe his quarry had taken another path and Cal had missed it. For a moment he was near panic; he felt as if he was lost irrevocably in the bowels of the earth. He stopped again. The air was foetid and his breathing was getting laboured.

He heard a noise up ahead. It sounded like metal striking against stone. He tiptoed onwards and suddenly turned a corner and saw a glimmer of light ahead. He got nearer and the light flickered on the walls and he knew it came from a torch.

At first he was surprised. Then he thought maybe the man ahead had figured he had only one pursuer and that one was already out of the running. Maybe he had not heard Cal's stealthy approach.

He negotiated a bend and the passage opened out and there, crouching in the light of a wall torch, was The Wolf. He had his back to Cal. But there was no mistaking those broad shoulders, that unnaturally-long unkempt black hair. He was digging with his hands at soft soil in a corner. He dragged a small sack out of the hole.

Cal levelled his gun. 'Get your hands up, pardner,' he said.

The man turned his head slowly. Then his movements speeded up, his hand rose, a handful of soil was flung upwards at Cal's face. The young man's finger contracted on the trigger. Even as the gun boomed he knew he had missed. He clawed at his stinging eyes, throwing himself forward as he did so.

He was as tall as The Wolf, though perhaps not so heavy. They collided with each other at top-speed and collapsed on the rock floor in a fighting heap.

Cal's elbow jarred against the hard surface and his gun spun from his hand. A knee ground into his stomach, knocking the wind out of him. Savage eyes glared into his. He got his arm loose, drove a fist upwards. He felt savage satisfaction as his knuckles grated on bone. A gun boomed in his ear. Rock-chips stung his face. Somehow he managed to get hold of The Wolf's gun-hand. They struggled for the weapon. Blood dripped from The Wolf's face on to Cal's hand.

Still struggling, the two men rose to their knees then to their feet. Cal gave a superhuman jerk on The Wolf's arm, making him release the gun. It went off again as it hit the floor, awakening hideous echoes in the enclosed space. The slug ricocheted from the rock-wall and whined away into the stillness.

Cal broke away from his opponent, regained his balance, swung a mighty fist. The Wolf was already dodging, but the blow caught him on the shoulder, spinning him round. He staggered against the wall. There was something strange about his head. His lank black hair was queerly lopsided. His face had been washed piebald by the rain and now, in the torchlight, a scar was blazed upon it.

The rage that surged through Cal Mackey was something the like of which he had never felt before. He sprang at his foe, his hands clawing upwards. The Wolf's black hair came away in his hands.

157

A fist smashing into his mouth sent Cal backwards. The wall held him up. Breathing heavily, he faced his greatest enemy, the big man with the scar, the man he had sworn to kill with his bare hands.

He launched himself forward again. Blows rained upon him but he hardly felt them – and finally, he got his hands around his enemy's throat and bore him back and pressed, and pressed. . . .

There was a roaring in his ears. A mist of blood swam before his eyes.

Hands grasped his shoulders, drew him upwards. He fought them off – until the familiar voice impinged on his ears.

'Take it easy, son,' said Pecos Charlie. 'Leave somep'n for the hangman.'

Cal let himself fall in a sitting position against the wall and looked about him. They were all coming into his view now. Verez was there, and Nevada and Brutus, and Matu and Biddy. All his friends. The old and the new. He wished with all his heart that Fin Bornwood could have been here, too, here at the end of the trail. Nevada held the sack containing the Government money. Such a little bundle to cause such a lot of grief and hate and hardship and death.

The torchlight danced crazily on the walls, the cave began to spin around him. Next moment Biddy was at his side, her cool hands on his flesh.

Brutus Calhoun, gunfighter and preacher, stood a little apart from the rest, leaning against the wall. He let his gun slide gently back into his holster. Soon he would be taking it away altogether, gunbelt and all.

The job was finished: he was a man of peace again.

They could go back home, those of them that were left. They could go back to Fort Bravo, all of them, Biddy too, maybe. It would be good for all of them if Biddy came back, too; but it would be particularly good for Cal Mackey, judging by the way the girl was looking at him now as she tended his wounds.